WE WILL TELL YOU OTHER- WISE

WE WILL TELL YOU OTHER-WISE

Beth Mayer

Black Lawrence Press

Black
Lawrence
Press

www.blacklawrence.com

Executive Editor: Diane Goettel
Cover Design: Zoe Norvell
Book Design: Amy Freels

Published 2019 by Black Lawrence Press.
Printed in the United States.

For Paul

CONTENTS

DON'T TELL YOUR MOTHER

There are three things you need to be a smelt fisherman: a net, a bucket, and your thumb.

There is only one thing you need to be a cadaver, and that's to be dead. My father and I had gone smelt fishing each spring ever since I'd turned seven. Now it was 1972, I was a boy of ten, and Richard Nixon had just been reelected president. We didn't know then what would happen with my mother's newest lump. My father was a doctor, and I'd been pestering him to let me see a real dead person, but he wasn't sure that was a good idea. My mother had always said yes to the smelt fishing, but she stayed home when we went, so she didn't have a chance to say anything about the cadaver.

Every time, we'd make the drive into Chicago before dark and park on Lakeshore Drive, just south of Navy Pier. Other fishermen would already be on the shore, sitting on overturned pickle buckets, holding their nets, and drinking beer. I would carry our bucket, stuffed with the net, and my father would carry our lawn chairs, the ones we never actually used on our lawn.

But on this trip, when we got to the breakwater, my father couldn't decide where to put the chairs. I could see how much he wanted to sit in one of the fishermen's circles, even though he disguised this as a friendly wink at me. They didn't know us, and we didn't know them, my father told me, but these good folks were the ones who came to the lake to catch their dinner, these good folks who didn't have money for things like lawn chairs or piano lessons or station wagons to take them to baseball practice.

I would have sat with them, no problem. They seemed fine to me, laughing a lot or just sitting back and looking out over Lake Michigan without clearing their throats to take up the silence.

That night we sat closer than we ever had before, just at the edge of one of their circles, around a fire burning yellow and red in an oil drum. We could hear a man in a brown coat telling a story about a one-eyed cat that honest-to-God predicted the future.

My father smiled at me, which meant, *You see, son? This is real life, here. This is what I'm talking about. Isn't this better than television?* And I smiled back at him because it *was* better than television.

We dropped our nets into the water, knowing the smelt would swim the same direction they always do and that before they could warn their family and friends a few rows back, everyone they knew and loved would crash into the net along with them. Then we raised the net, heavy with all those smelt, and picked them out one by one. Some were as small as my little finger, some as big as a small perch. Their size didn't matter. We popped their heads off—*Snap! Snap!*—squeezing them between our thumbs and index fingers. Then we scooped our thumbs into the holes where their heads were supposed to be and gutted them clean.

We always waited to eat until we were back home. My father would cook the smelt in a cast-iron skillet, and when they were per-fectly browned, we would pop the whole smelt—tail, scales, and all—right into our mouths. But that night we didn't go home, and my father kept moving our chairs closer to the circle. Everyone kept on fishing and drinking and talking, except I was right there with them and everything felt different. The man in the brown coat invited us to cook our smelt over his fire. It was warm around the fire, and I liked the sizzle smell and the slow, steady way we ate them, smelt after smelt after smelt.

After a while a man who looked like a woman, with a small, soft face and thin wrists, stood up and handed my father a bottle of beer.

The man's hand was red raw, with dirt and blood packed under long fingernails. My father did not keep staring at that hand the way I did but looked up into the man's eyes and said, "Thanks much," then took a long swig of the beer.

We sat and fished and ate and my father told some stories I had never heard before. One time, when he was a boy, his grandfather aimed a pistol through the living room window and shot a porcupine off the cab of his truck. Another time, long ago, his cousin Mike went swinging from a rope into Cold Lake and never came up again.

The man in the brown coat said, "Cousin of mine: same damn thing, different lake."

Then the man in the brown coat told us about his mother, her brown-sugar ham and blue-flowered housedress and the prize-winning tomatoes in her garden.

"That was down in Carolina," he said. "Mind you, everything grows in Carolina."

I wanted to say something, too, so I asked, "Which Carolina, North or South?"

The man who looked like a woman put his arm around the man in the brown coat's shoulder, leaned in, and giggled. Then he said, "Why South, boy! It's gotta be South!"

It was getting late when we heard a man in another circle raise his voice: "Get the hell out here, Marty."

The man in the brown coat got up, saying, "I'd better go see about this."

The man who looked like a woman said, "Sit your ass down, Georgie-Pie."

So now the man in the brown coat was Georgie-Pie, and Georgie-Pie laughed and walked toward the arguing men anyway. Our circle went on eating and drinking, but we were quiet now. We were listening.

The loud man said, "I don't owe you shit, Marty, and you know it." Then the other man, Marty, said something that none of us could make out.

The loud man was getting louder: "You think you gotta claim, here? You think you gotta *claim*?" My father turned his chair, and I watched him keeping an eye on the men in the light of the fires.

The man who looked like a woman said softly, "Georgie-Pie," but we all knew that Georgie-Pie couldn't hear it. Georgie-Pie stepped between the two men and gripped their shoulders, turning to face one, then the other. He told them something in a low voice about no need, no need.

"You see this, George? Can you believe this shit?" said the loud man.

My father told me this was not good. He wanted to take me home. He said we would just leave our fishing gear right where it was, and when he said "Go" we would go quickly, heading away from the commotion, even though we'd have to cut back to get to the car.

I was ready for my father's signal, but before he could say the word, we heard Georgie-Pie cry out, "Ohhh," and saw him slump to the ground. Marty was the one to go, fast, running into the night. I heard the loud man shout, "George!" The man who looked like a woman moved toward him, saying, "Darling, Darling," and crouched where Georgie-Pie was curling up.

My father told me to hand him my coat, then went straight to Georgie-Pie. I followed him, and stumbled over a pickle bucket. My father knelt down next to Georgie-Pie and told him, "Don't worry, I'm a doctor." Then he lifted Georgie-Pie's head, placed my coat under his neck, pulled up Georgie-Pie's blood-soaked T-shirt and searched the skin on his belly. I watched closely as my father put his hands into Georgie-Pie's stomach right where the blade had gone in.

My father sent me for help, and I heard myself repeating every word that he told me to say, one word for every step I ran. And I ran like a ballplayer rounding third base and headed for home, like a silver smelt trying to reach the shore. I ran until I reached the lit curb, stepped into the phone booth, dialed the operator, and spilled every word into the mouth-piece: "There has been a stabbing at the breakwater near Navy Pier, and we need an ambulance immediately for one conscious male victim, age forty-five, who is in the care of a surgeon from Mercy Hospital. The attacker fled but alert the police that his name is Marty, and he was last seen running near the pier."

Back at the water's edge, I saw my father with his hands still inside the hole in Georgie-Pie's stomach. There was blood on my father's arms, but the bleeding had stopped. My father said, "All right, my friend, you're going to be just fine."

"Just *fine*," he said again, this time directly to the man who looked like a woman.

Then, to me, my father said, "Son, are you alright?" I could only nod my head, because suddenly I felt like I could cry, and I didn't want that. I wanted to be ready for anything. The loud man and the man who looked like a woman both thanked my father. They thanked him and thanked him, and then they thanked God.

It took nine minutes for the ambulance to get there, and my father told the paramedics they sure took their sweet time. He would not take his hands out of Georgie-Pie, not until there was a stretcher under Georgie-Pie's back and a needle in his arm and a white cotton blanket pulled up to his waist, not until a paramedic presented a sealed IV bag and a small metal clamp, which he held up for my father. "Satisfied?" he asked.

Then my father said, "OK. Take this fellow to Mercy. Not Cook County, Mercy. Under the care of Dr. Morrison. He's on tonight."

The paramedic agreed but said he couldn't let any of these people ride in the ambulance. When my father said what the hell, the paramedic said policy is policy and to take it up with his boss.

After Georgie-Pie and the ambulance had gone, the loud man and the man who looked like a woman told us, "We know the way to Mercy. It's late. You just get your boy home."

In the car, I thought about my father and me almost leaving too soon. I thought about my mother, waiting for us at home. I thought about quick jabs with sharp knives, where we go if we never wake up, and Georgie-Pie.

"I want to go to Mercy, too," I told my father.

"Son," my father started to say.

"We have to make sure he's all right," I said. "We *have* to." And my father turned the car around.

At Mercy, my father talked with Dr. Morrison, and we found the loud man and the man who looked like a woman in the waiting room, drinking cups of black coffee.

They stood up, and my father told them, "George is resting now. He looks very good."

"Can we take him?" asked the man who looked like a woman.

"Not yet," my father said. "He needs to be monitored to make sure there's no sign of infection. He should go home tomorrow."

The loud man said, "Well, we don't know what to say."

We all shook hands and wished each other well. When my father and I got to the elevator he told me there was something he wanted me to see.

"But please don't tell your mother," he said, "it might upset her." And I understood.

We went down to the basement, and that's where my father showed me the cadaver. His name was John Doe. My father and I put on masks and gloves and stood next to John Doe. Then my father said, "I'm sorry, son," but I didn't know if he meant the long night, or John Doe, or the new lump in my mother's breast. I wanted to tell my father how glad I was for the night, how good it felt to save somebody.

Then he asked me if I thought it was time to put John Doe away, and it was.

TELL ME SOMETHING I DON'T KNOW

This weekend, my mother is flying in to give me and Lora a break. *For your sanity*, my mother tells me, *for your marriage.* My son, Ethan, has a brain tumor. It's likely going to kill him eventually. For now, it's Ethan's job to have cancer and my wife's job to take care of Ethan.

We had other plans, as one does. Lora is fluent in German and has her master's degree in art history. We met when I was in law school and she was a graduate student where we practiced having combative sex until I asked her to marry me. It took a year before she finally said yes. Actually, she said: OK. You win.

She has always been beautiful. To me, it seems effortless, but apparently there are three ounce jars of cosmo-pharmaceutical serum for two hundred and fifty dollars that promise to keep a woman's skin youthful and dewy. Is this common knowledge? When I tell Lora that I think her laugh lines are sexy, I mean it. But she thinks that I am just being cheap. I don't say, "Listen. You can probably lay off the serum since you don't laugh much these days." Ba-dum-dum. This little ditty I keep to myself. I know it's not funny. You think I'm an asshole? I just miss my wife.

Ethan has chemo every other Thursday. Lora sits next to him in a pleather recliner that she would never allow in our house. A young nurse's aide wears a Pepto-Bismol pink smock adorned with charming turtles. She hands Ethan an iPad to pick out a G-rated movie, which then appears on a big-screen TV on the wall. A world of obedient screens is the only one that Ethan has ever known. He gets whatever he wants with a tap on his small index finger. Really, that can't be good for a person, can it? We set limits on screen time. We play *Uno* and *Jenga* and hide the television remote. Walt Disney's lackeys have a corner on the G-rated market and Ethan's latest obsession is *Bambi*. This means, for the foreseeable future, he will watch *Bambi*—and only *Bambi*—during chemo and at home, too. He has all the lines memorized and knows the plot by heart.

I need to take that kid to a real God-damned baseball game. In the spring. After the season starts. When his counts are good. I don't care how the Cubs are playing, or who. We'll chow down on nitrate-laden hotdogs, a beer for me and a real Coca-Cola in a plastic souvenir cup for Ethan to keep. Lora could come along, too. For the spectacle. Maybe we'll see a pair of twenty-somethings on the Jumbo-Tron kiss for the camera.

After chemo, Ethan says: Poor Bambi! His mom and dad are dead. Now he's all alone. My wife looks at me. Raises one eyebrow. She translates most of Ethan's observations into some ominous sub-text like a fatalistic linguist. I say: Well? The kid's right. I remind her that at least *Bambi* is not *The Little Mermaid*. At least we seem to be done with *The Little Mermaid*. You have to count your blessings. Or pick your poison. And for God's sake, not *every* single thing means some other terrible thing. But that I keep to myself.

I forget to pick my mother up at the airport. I don't even remember that I forgot her until she is standing in our entryway. She took a cab, no bother. Hands me a $50 gift card to The Olive Garden, a gift for me and Lora, when I start to apologize. My mother says: don't worry, honey, you have so much on your mind.

When I graduated from law school, my mother gave me the following marching orders: *choose to be happy*. She was from the Midwest, the flyover region of my youth that I had swiftly—but temporarily—disavowed on my way to becoming a public defender. My mother did not read the *New York Times*. My mother was embarrassing and provincial. Choose to be happy? Right. That was a luxury afforded only the uninformed and foolish.

Lora reminds me that she doesn't like The Olive Garden. But my mother has come all this way, I say. It will hurt her feelings if we don't go. Lora thinks that Ethan is having a bad day. Just for an hour, I say. Lora frowns. She's not really hungry. Then a walk? We could re-gift the card later to one of Ethan's nurses. Lora has already walked for an hour on the treadmill while Ethan watched *Bambi*. I was in the next room. Don't I remember? A half hour. Can't we just get out of this house at the same time and just sit across a fucking table from each other for a half an hour? Lora tells me Ethan. It's just. Ethan.

Once upon a time, Lora was a straight cis-female, but now she self-identifies as "mom-of-a-terminal-kid." When she is not taking care of Ethan, she frequents these bullshit blogs full of saccharine mantras and cherubic-angel-kiddos holding court in the clouds. They are her porn. Now, she offers to read me something that she found. This special thought from her to me. Face to face. Her best offer at intimacy in such a long time, I listen.

To the whole house, I call out: I'm getting carryout from The Olive Garden.

When I am almost home with dinner, I really want a cigarette. But Lora and I both quit when Ethan was born. I don't want a fight when I get home and she gets a whiff. At the 7-Eleven gas station three blocks away from our house, I buy a tin of cherry-flavored chewing tobacco. Same terrible shit that I started on when I was thirteen.

I walk across the street to Ethan's elementary school. On the playground, I sit on a sturdy platform that leads to another sturdy platform. There is a friendly ramp, a thick pole to slide down. Every surface is coated in something non-toxic. I kick at the carpet of woodchips, pick one up, sniff for a hit of cedar. But it's not real. They are rubberized imposters, designed to soften a multitude of inevitable falls. I spit tobacco juice down at my feet, the color is a match. The truth is, Lora has always been pretty skilled at being miserable. Ethan's brain tumor has just given her the chance to get better at it.

Apparently, Ethan likes The Olive Garden just fine. My mother is not the least bit surprised. Outside our picture window, the sun is getting low. My mother and I play cards with Ethan. When it is time for bed, Lora reads him two stories and falls asleep in the spare bed in Ethan's room.

When Lora is out running errands, I hand Ethan the clicker. Tell him: have at it, kid! Then we wink at each other. I don't mind that he watches the same movies over and over again until Lora gets home and tells us both *enough!*

Parents are only as happy as their unhappiest kid. That is what Lora had to say, what she wanted me to understand. But my wife didn't really need to tell me that, because I already knew.

When everyone in the house is finally asleep, I step outside. It is fall in the Midwest and sometimes that means the air is made of silk. My feet bare on the concrete driveway, the night feels good against my skin. Almost like a secret human touch.

WHEN THE SAINTS TELL THEIR OWN

The night before Blue took the number eleven bus to Central Hospital, Saint Joan of Arc visited me again and told me to give Mother's old paisley curtains to Mrs. Duffy. The real problem with Blue has nothing to do with his brain. The real problem with Blue is that he is eight and has yet to find his true calling. No one in our house sleeps much, so Blue's not special. It would have been a night like any other.

In the morning, Mother and Father and I were retrieving our coffee in the kitchen and hadn't noticed Blue was gone. The telephone rang at six and Mother answered.

"Yes. I see. Of course."

"What is it?" Father asked.

"We'll be there in fifteen minutes," Mother said to the phone.

Father wiped his hands on his slacks, waiting.

She told us, "It seems Blue took the bus to Central Hospital this morning and asked the volunteer at the welcome desk how a person might go about being admitted to the psychiatric ward."

Father and I didn't know what came next. We looked to Mother, the way we always looked to Mother. She stood there with her impressive stance.

"Well, we're to go to the hospital," she said. "We need to bring him home."

Mother and Father sat beside each other in the front seats. We didn't take drives and on the way to the hospital the back of their heads confounded me. Long ago, Mother and Father had quite a love affair. Once, Mother told me about the way Father used to try to make her favorite things—complicated endeavors like the perfect tomato bisque. The way he followed her, from city to sit-in, just to be with her. And another time, Father told me that he had fallen hard for my mother. How could he not, he said, with her heart for justice, her aversion to modern dance, her clarity of thought? I liked to imagine that I knew her then. There were polls in Alabama, organic farming, sit-ins. And we were friends. I imagined what we would have talked about when Mother still believed in fighting for the flawed and miserable world. I would pray, she would march.

But I was sure that Mother and Father were no longer lovers. Neither would I call them companions. They were loyal, working in service to their separate ambitions by staying out of the other's way. Blue and I were simply to do the same.

When we arrived at the hospital, Blue was asleep in a small recliner in the social worker's office. The door was slightly open and the social worker was waiting for us just outside. After the introductions, the social worker tried apologizing for Blue.

"He must be just exhausted."

"Of course," Mother said. Mother was being extremely polite.

"Do you mind if we just let him rest, then, and sit here a moment?" The social worker gestured to four chairs lined up in the hall near her office.

"That would be fine," Mother said. Father remained standing.

The social worker looked down at her papers.

"Let's just gather some basic information first, if you don't mind."

"Certainly," Mother said, "go right ahead."

What did she need to know to fill in her blanks? I could tell her if she asked me. Blue's shining mind had failed him now, or at least he was convinced that it had. This fact might present an actual problem, as Mother revered a strong cerebellum the way she once had faith in abstract and noble things. Back when I was just twelve and Blue was only three, Mother asked an old college friend to run the standard intelligence quotient tests on us. I remember replicating geometrical shapes using red blocks. In return, Mother made her friend a set of green nesting bowls. Then she locked our IQs away in a safety deposit box at the credit union. Last year, when I had wanted specifics, Mother told me: rest-assured-you-and-Blue-are-both-well-endowed-in-all-things-cognitive-now-get-on-with-it.

What the social worker actually wanted to know was this: were Mother and Father Blue's biological parents and legal guardians; Blue's date of birth; height and weight; home address; phone number; another number where they might be reached; siblings; surgeries or hospitalizations; any allergies to drugs or medications that they were aware of? That was all she needed for now.

"Very good," the social worker said, "on to Blue's—arrival." She looked first at Mother, then Father, and then for a moment, she kept her eyes on me. "You understand, of course, that this is highly unusual."

"Is it?" Mother said.

The social worker sat up, straight.

"Yes, it is. First, I must ask you. Do you have any concerns regarding your son's safety? Do you believe that he is a danger to himself or others?"

"Danger?" Mother said, "I should say not!" Mother was doing her best, keeping her passion in check. Then she turned to Father. Father had nothing to add.

"No, we have no concerns."

"You see, Blue seems convinced that there is something terribly wrong with him," the social worker said.

Mother said nothing.

"We would certainly like to be of help. Make a referral. You understand." Now the social worker was looking at me. "Perhaps your daughter has noticed some behavioral or mood changes?"

I knew of Blue's penchant for collecting remnants. He saved odd things, items that we had used like discarded tea bags, notes, tissues. When Blue had gathered enough, he shaped the pieces into abstract collages and taped them to his bedroom wall. But this was nothing new.

Blue also loved to fish. That was something. And to be kind I had let him take me carp fishing a few weeks—or had it been months?— back. Maybe there had been some indication of his pending break-down then, but I had missed it. Blue had taken me to Grassy River. There we saw two grown men and a boy standing in the water, sitting in a lawn chair and digging at the hard dirt with a stick respectively. Blue had cocked his head toward the old man in the lawn chair and said, "He reminds me of me."

Perhaps I could tell the social worker this at least. That my brother and I had something in common. Feeling old, that is.

Or that Blue usually lugged around a toolbox he had found by the tracks. When I had asked him what was inside, he squatted low near the gray box to show me. Inside was a block of Styrofoam, three even rows of small metal hooks and two spools of clear fishing line, bound together with a fat rubber band. I suppose Blue was meticulous about such things. But not to a pathological degree! Under the lid, he had taped an old black and white photograph of Mother and Father. They were standing together on the edge of a large crowd. Mother's thick braid rested across one shoulder. She was leaning hard into Father, his arm tight around her small waist. Blue preserved this relic among his treasures and I wanted nothing more than to rip it to shreds.

But how to say any of this to a stranger? And to what end?

The social worker indicated that she was still waiting for me.

"Sarah is it?" I could see my full name there in front of her, in writing.

Mother and Father christened me Summer because I was born in the heart of winter, the offspring of their irony. At fifteen I became—with their permission—first, a Catholic, and then Sarah Michael Regina in my hopes of becoming a Bride of Christ. Father was intrigued by my conversion and Mother found it simply amusing.

"Sarah Michael," I told the social worker. "I go by both names." How I wanted to pinch her lips together!

"Oh, yes. I see that here now, Sarah Michael. Any observations about Blue that you would like to share?"

Blue was bored. I was a late bloomer, not unlike Blue, I suppose. I shouldn't be so hasty. Maybe my brother needed some help discerning what to do with all of his time. My nights were long, too, before my dear saints arrived. I imagined Blue sitting there alone on our front step, his fishing things beside him, and waiting for the sun. I knew that I had been fasting for a while. I have some regrets. I wanted to tell Blue that I was sorry to have missed it. I should have reminded him where the encyclopedias and almanacs were shelved!

All this. But what I heard myself say: "Blue is lonely."

"Really?" the social worker asked. Father was shifting.

Mother said, "I'm not sure that this is appropriate." I could see that the social worker didn't understand.

"But it's only because he's still so young," I said.

The social worker's eyebrows looked pleased and she leaned in toward me. She wanted more. "Tell me about that."

What could I tell? No one slept much. Father spends the moonlight hours studying his William Blake and goes on examining the Illuminated Works. Plate by plate, it's "Ghost of Abel" and "Urizen" and all the rest. Father doesn't actually believe in Blake or God for that matter. What turns him on about Blake is the paradox: how true genius can be born from such misguided convictions. Father has made Blake his life's work, but in the end it's all just stuff and fluff to Father.

Mother you can find down in her basement studio. But don't interrupt her at the wheel! She's making her clay things. If they are not exactly right, she can smash them to bits and move on.

As for me, Saint Joan of Arc and Saint Catherine began to arrive soon after my conversion, and thus began my (fruitful!) vigil for the seen and the unseen. I almost always find it best to keep these details to myself and told the social worker nothing.

Mother stepped in, though. "Well, now. I suppose it's true that Blue hasn't been sleeping very well."

Wasn't Blue in real trouble now and wasn't Mother bearing false witness against our neighbor the social worker? The Benedictines had told me time and again that however accurate (they allowed) I might be, it was still not my commission to ascertain, condemn, or forgive the sins of others. Still, in this case before me, I wasn't sure whether Mother was breaking Number Eight if she had convinced even herself that she spoke the truth.

The social worker was busy taking notes. "Right. A childhood sleep disturbance for Blue then. I see. Any nightmares? Bedwetting? Allergies?"

Oh, but Mother was finished with this! "We'll be sure to consult our pediatrician. I'm certain it will pass. We'll be taking Blue home now."

"Yes, of course. We just want to be of some help. To Blue." The social worker was looking to me again. "And the family unit."

The social worker was being ironic. She was being witty! I knew my Latin: "family" (one word) and then "unit" from the Latin "unus," earlier being *unity*. It just struck me, and I had to laugh. The social worker did not join me, but rather frowned. She was not joking and may not have been familiar with the etymology of the phrase after all. I knew that our family dynamics were unique unto themselves. Did the social worker not see this? Perhaps she thought we were sitting around together in the evening playing board games? She was a fool.

Father went to Blue then, and lifted Blue up into his long arms. An almost recognizable ache began in the center of my chest and I covered it up with my hand. Blue did not wake on the way home or after Mother laid him on top of his bed or when I covered him up with my quilt. Lunch was tomato sandwiches, and no Blue.

After dinner, Mother went down to her basement studio and Father went up to study his Blake. Father's sound in the house: an occasional steady thwap, the turning of a page. Mother's: the humming wheel and the thick sound of wet clay being thrown down to begin or start over, again.

Visiting the sick is a corporal work of mercy and Blue was the closest thing to sick that I had ever known. I pulled Blue's desk chair beside his bed and began to read Saint Thomas on the Seven Deadlies. The sky and then Blue's room began to darken. I hoped that my dear saints would know where to find me. I turned on Blue's reading lamp. Tomorrow was a Wednesday, and almost every Wednesday I walk the Labyrinth at the Benedictine Center at four. The nature of any Labyrinth is to arrive back at the exact same place you started. Everyone is welcome: businessmen and women, looking for a spiritual fix, and tourists using the ancient maze as an elevated form of recreation. My Sisters were my favorite company, strolling arm and arm. Once I had even seen our own neighbor, Mrs. Duffy, walking ahead of me. She didn't wave, but I knew Mrs. Duffy by the slope of her back.

I remembered my charge to safely deliver the paisley curtains to Mrs. Duffy. Helping a neighbor was a charitable deed, and Blue would have understood had he been awake. The curtains were in the guest room in a storage chest covered in plastic. I removed the plastic and folded them nicely and placed them in a wicker laundry basket. It was almost midnight when I rang Mrs. Duffy's doorbell. I would apologize for the late hour, but when Mrs. Duffy saw these paisley curtains all would be forgiven. I imagined them hanging in her dining room, the table set with china and silver. My vision grew, and there were Mother and Father and Blue all sitting down together waiting for Mrs. Duffy and me to join them. It was an improbable scene, but on a day like today, with these curtains finally where they truly belonged, who could say? The door opened and a strange man stood before me in nothing but his cotton pajamas.

"Yes?" he asked. I had thought Mrs. Duffy lived alone, but I wasn't sure.

"I'm sorry it is so late," I said. This man was too young to be Mrs. Duffy's husband.

"Yes. It is quite late. Can I help you with something?" I didn't like this.

"I've brought these for Mrs. Duffy." I raised my basket to show him. I find it wise to keep my visitations and subsequent assignments to myself, so I told the man, "These are some paisley curtains she admired once. For her dining room." He looked unclear. "Or wherever she likes." The man lowered his head, and stood blocking the doorway. Who was this man? Where was Mrs. Duffy? "But you see, I must give them to her myself." I needed to get inside. "I think she'll be quite pleased."

"I'm sorry," the man said. He reached toward me, and I stepped back. "I don't know what to say. The curtains are lovely. Obviously, you haven't heard. My mother, Mrs. Duffy, passed away two weeks ago. I'm just staying a few more days until her affairs are in order."

No. Saint Joan had been specific. Helping a neighbor was a charitable deed.

"It's very late," he said, "and I appreciate you thinking of my mother." He was closing the door! "Good night."

What could I do? I left the basket on Mrs. Duffy's front steps, my best effort at obedience. Next time, Saint Joan would certainly catch it from me.

Mrs. Duffy used to be alive next door. Back upstairs, Blue slept. In his dark room, I tipped Blue's reading lamp toward my page. When I came upon the deadly sin of Sloth, I began to skim. I feared no laziness under our roof! *Tristitia de bono spirituali.* No, no, no. Not sloth in the conventional sense, but an ancient meaning. *Tristitia de bono spirituali?* None of my saints came to enlighten me. I leaned in toward Blue's small face and he surprised me with a noisy sigh that tasted like maple syrup. *Tristitia de bono spirituali.* Sadness in the face of spiritual good. Turning away from joy. I traced the passage, slowly, with my index finger. With the illuminated bones of my own finger—being ordered, from age to age, the distal, the middle, and the proximal phalanges.

Like Blue's bones or my own bones or any other saint's bones.

Here was Blue's sweet and steady breath. Here, my new vigil. Right beside my brother's bed. Right where I would be when he was sure to wake in the morning.

DARLING, WON'T YOU TELL ME TRUE?

Auctioneer's Notebook, dated August 9, 1987: From private letters (wrapped in blue organza) recovered from the Harrington's attic trunk. Not to be auctioned with the estate.
June 11, 1956
Dear Mrs. Christopher,

I hope that you will not find me completely lacking in sentimentality, but given the nature of the present situation, I must be frank. Mother's passing was not a disappointment and her things are of no consequence to me now. As her most trusted caregiver for the last eight years, I understand that you will be managing her estate and for that I am most grateful to you. Please see that you are compensated according to your usual arrangement; I am certain that mother would have wished as much.

Respectfully,
Mr. James
Harrington

June 31, 1956

Dear Miss Christopher,

Thank you for your timely response and for clarifying your marital status. You seem to be a lady who can appreciate that one must be sensitive to such formalities. As to your question regarding compensation, might I suggest that you receive your hourly rate plus any overtime, mileage, or expenses that you incur? Though I must confess that my law practice has been quiet these last few months, I am afraid I cannot see my way home to assist you with mother's affairs. Please do not hesitate to write again should the need arise.

Respectfully,

James Harrington,

Esquire

July 15, 1956

Dear Miss Christopher,

I did not realize that mother had acquired quite so many cats. I agree completely, it would be a shame to see all seven of them put down. You are very kind. Of course, they may be parceled out among your cat loving friends and family members. I myself am allergic. As to mother's ripe or ripening vegetables, mother never kept any sort of garden in my youth. (Just when did she take this up, I wonder?) In the last several years I have developed my own knack for gardening. I am more patient now. And you are quite right once again, Miss Christopher. Such a bountiful harvest ought not go to waste. If you are so inclined, please feel free to water, weed and pick according to the rest of the season. Keep track of your hours, of course.

Sincerely,

James Harrington

August 7, 1956
Dear Sarah,

Thank you for inviting me to address you as such. And please, you may call me James. Mr. Sorenson from Minneapolis sounds fine. Although it's a pity you couldn't have found a nice fellow from Hudson to help you. Anyway, Mr. Sorenson's suggestion rings true enough; a few small pieces from mother's collection going to the Phipps Center would be nice. Mother would have relished having a nameplate or two, wouldn't she?

Regarding the proceeds from the auction, the list of organizations you mentioned are excellent. (Junior League, Smith College, et al.) I was surprised to learn that, ever since you've known her, mother was an active member in all her philanthropic endeavors. Were you sorry to hear my news that mother used to be a joiner in namesake only? Perhaps you knew a softer version of mother than I. I confess that I had no idea how much work this would be. I do hope that it is not proving too taxing. Please keep me abreast of your progress. And do let me know when Mr. Sorenson finishes his work at the house.

Sincerely,
James

September 21, 1956
Dear Sarah,

I am quite troubled at the notion of Mr. Sorenson setting up a sleeping cot on the screen porch. The drive from Minneapolis to Hudson does not seem to warrant this peculiar measure. But I suppose if you feel comfortable with his intentions, it may speed things along. No, your questions regarding mother and me are not too familiar. I am heartened to know that someone truly cared for her. I hope you don't think me a beast. A boy doesn't set out to dislike his mother. First and foremost, mother was a collector. She was busy acquiring various items, to the point of obsession, in any given year. I most clearly recall: her oil painting phase, her Chinese pottery stint, and her equestrian period. Remembering this just now, I confess that the latter was of particular difficultly for me. How I desperately wanted to ride! But mother wouldn't hear of it. She boarded every horse with its own trainer, for show and for profit. Of course you are right: a mother's passing is always a loss. I understand that this is the natural way. I do wish I felt it more. And I am deeply sorry that you never knew your own mother. I am beginning to wonder if I ever knew mine. Mother was, somehow, too distant and still too familiar. I do not understand how this contradiction can stand, but it was my world. Before bed, mother whispered to me details that a boy doesn't want to know. (Perhaps I say too much, Sarah. Forgive me?) By day, though, I sought mother out. I followed her around like an eager little pup until it occurred to me one afternoon that I was a bother. I believe it was a Wednesday, because I had piano.

I do regret that going through all of mother's things with Mr. Sorenson is taking quite so long.

Sincerely,

James

September 27, 1956

Dear Sarah,

I do not believe Mr. Sorenson ought to move upstairs to one of the guest rooms. To be candid with you, I think it rather brazen of him to ask. Please be wary of him. If he is chilly at night on the porch, why don't you offer him a few of mother's old quilts? Frankly, the man does not seem all that efficient at his work.

James

October 9, 1956
Dear Sarah,

I am glad the situation is resolved to your liking. Mr. Sorenson should be fine remaining where he is, and perhaps the impending fall weather will inspire him finish his duties in a more timely manner. I do remember the small profile silhouette you mentioned. Yes, that is me as a boy. I believe I was seven or eight. As I recall, mother had the artist edit my nose a bit to make it more cherub-like. Of course, you are not too bold to ask. By all means you may have it, if it pleases you.

Sincerely,
James

October 23, 1956
Dear Sarah,

I am pleased to hear that the date of the auction has finally been set. But why is Mr. Sorenson still at the house? Forgive me, but I am afraid he is becoming too familiar with you. If my schedule permits, I would like to attend the auction to see that all goes well. You have done an outstanding job with mother's affairs. I hope you will understand my motives and trust this gesture will not be seen as intrusive. I will arrange to stay at the home of an old classmate of mine and will send word soon of my arrival plans.

Sincerely,
James

November 1, 1956

Dear Sarah,

Though it will be strange to stay at mother's after all these years, I thank you. I am glad you suggested that I take one of the guest rooms. It does make perfect sense. I confess that I am very pleased our lazy Mr. So and So has finally packed to go. I was beginning to loathe him. He is not very handsome, is he? I am not at all handsome, I'm afraid. Do you care about such things? I look forward to meeting you within the week. I am glad to find within myself some comfort knowing that mother spent her last days with you. As to your charming litany of questions: My train is scheduled to arrive at two and, if it's on time, that should put me at the house around three. Any room will do. You choose. But don't worry yourself, please, don't go to any trouble. Yes, some apple cobbler would be lovely when I arrive. I haven't tasted it in so many years, I had almost forgotten about it. And no, just the one cat shouldn't cause me too much distress.

Fondly,

James

after Lisa Franker's "What's Left at Low Tide" (gouache on book covers)

LET HER TELL THE WAY

In the summer of 1978, the whole family was supposed to go to Niagara Falls. Peggy Finch had started selling *Mary Kay*[1] cosmetics to her friends and neighbors, and her husband Frank insisted that she keep every dollar. He called it her "pink money" because everything that *Mary Kay* sold was packaged in pink. Her husband was the owner-operator of a funeral home going back three generations, and his hobby was planning vacations for his family that never happened.

The day before their scheduled departure, Frank explained to Peggy and the children that, once again, their travel plans had been thwarted by the unexpected. Someone, tragically, had died. He would definitely take them all to Niagara Falls next year. Or someplace even better.

But people *died*. That was to be expected, actually.

Peggy said, "What about Bill? He could help the Hendersons with their arrangements."

"But they've used us for years, Peggy. You know I couldn't do that to the Hendersons."

What he didn't say: he would do this, to them, instead. Peggy waited for the children to weigh in. Tiffany was the oldest. A teen. She was almost entirely self-absorbed and the family did not ask much from her any more.

---

1. A multi-level marketing company, geared toward homemakers and founded by Mary Kay Ash (1918–2001) in 1963 based ostensibly upon the principle "God first, family second, career third."

"Can I go upstairs now? And use the phone?" she said.

Ceci, the baby, was under the table poking at the cat. Randy was nine years old, forever the boy in the middle.

He spoke up, "That's alright Dad. It's not your fault."

For the rest of that day and into the evening Peggy was very, very quiet. After dinner, Frank said he needed to go out for a bit. Work, Peg thought. But soon her husband drove home in a surprise for her: the new Ford Country Squire[2] station wagon that she had been eyeing for months. He gave her the keys and a kiss.

"We'll go next year," he told her, "you'll see."

Peggy took the car. (An extravagant, ridiculous apology.) But it was a practical decision and not the same thing as forgiving him.

Once there was supposed to be a trip to the Grand Canyon, including an overnight on a small dairy farm in North Dakota with lanky third cousins the children hadn't met and Peggy recalled from a wedding long ago.

"You can milk a real cow," Frank had told the children.

"Don't they use machines for that now, Frank?" Peggy had asked.

"Well these work too," Frank said, raising his fists, tugging at imaginary teats.

There were times (used to be times) when the family felt as if they really had traveled somewhere together—the way memories and story gently accumulate to create meaning. Months before a trip, Frank conducted extensive research and composed well-informed inquiries to the Visitors' Bureau. When a package arrived, Frank gathered the family around the kitchen table and spread brochures and pamphlets (all color and bounty) like a feast before them.

---

2. The Country Squire was the premium full-size Ford station wagon, featuring imitation-wood trim on both the doors and tailgate.

Earlier that summer, Peggy's newly formed women's group was holding court in the living room when the older children had arrived home early from their Park & Rec program just in time to witness the ladies sitting in a circle with mirrors between their legs. (Peggy had been hoping for a ripe flower. An O'Keefe. A peony in bloom.) But the meeting adjourned abruptly, with rushed apologies out the front door. Randy seemed confounded.

"Don't you get it?" Tiffany told her brother, "They were looking down there." Randy still did not understand.

"You mean," he was not looking at his mother, but his sister, "at their crotches?"

Tiffany clarified, "At their naked crotches." The boy's face contorted and Tiffany seemed satisfied now.

"Tell me about it!" she said.

Peggy constructed for herself an equation, a formula working forward up until this moment. It involved time and age, privacy and ownership. She had not earned the girl's conviction here. "Tiffany," Peggy said, "that's enough."

On Saturday morning, the day that the family was supposed to leave for Niagara Falls, the children were in the family room watching "The Road Runner" and Peggy was slicing red apples. She had asked Frank to bring up a small cooler from the basement and felt him watching her.

"Picnic today?"

"No," Peggy said.

"Where are you headed?" Frank was still trying to make up.

She wasn't trying to be coy. She was afraid to say it, to hurt and anger him. "We're going, Frank."

"Going?" Now Frank was listening.

"On the family trip you planned. After breakfast." His face registered relief.

"Oh, Peggy," he moved toward her, put his arm around her. "Come on, we'll go next year." Peggy knew he was trying to soften her toward him. He didn't really think she would go. The fact that she had an old truth to present never changed anything.

"Frank, you know if you told the Hendersons about our vacation they would use Bill instead. They would be happy to."

"I can't do that," he said. He hung his head a bit and it was not for effect. Peggy knew exactly how her husband would choose. She knew the intricacies of his primary failings and companionable virtues.

"I know Frank, and I'm sorry." She meant this.

"That's better."

"No, Frank," Peggy said. He had not understood, "the kids and I, we are still going."

"In the car I bought you?" he said. (Oh, she felt foolish now. Tricked by the costly gift.)

"Frank! That isn't fair." He knew it.

"Well, besides that," his way of saying, yes, you're right, "What will you do for money?"

"I have money, remember?" Poor Frank. What could he do? He really was a mild man, a hard worker, simply grateful for Peggy's love. As a boy, he had been the son of the undertaker. The other children said he smelled like death and he had. They did not know the name for formaldehyde.

"Don't be ridiculous, Peggy. Niagara Falls is almost a ten-hour drive from here." Frank was grasping now.

"I know that."

"Well, that's great. Just great," he was pacing, agitated. "Best of luck. I sure hope you remember the number for AAA"[3] This exchange felt like a spiral, a whirlpool. Peggy just had to hold on. "I can't believe you're doing this to me."

---

3. American Automobile Association; fee-based membership provides services including maps and roadside assistance. Commonly believed that AAA can protect loyal members from flat tires, wrong turns, and acts of God.

"Oh, Frank," Peggy said. And her heart really did go out to him. "You are doing this, Frank. You."

Ten miles from home, Peggy said to the children, "Isn't this nice?" It was not really a question. Peggy caught Randy in the rearview. "Where's dad?" the boy said. He was testing her. Wasn't it good to shape a better truth for your children when necessary?

"Your father just couldn't get away," Peggy said. She turned on the stereo. Tiffany had the front passenger seat and, with that, her presumption as our deejay. The girl reached to turn the dial but Peggy touched her hand, "Wait, I like those Bee Gee brothers."

Tiffany produced a remarkable sound, equal parts growl and exaggerated sigh, "Mother, that's not even what they're called!" She wanted to listen to the Rolling Stones.

"That's not what they're called? What are they called?"

Randy said, "It's just 'The Bee Gees.' There is no 'brothers.'"

"Are we actually *talking* about this? Who cares?" Tiffany said.

Randy tried going into an *Encyclopedia Brown* mystery until he began to complain of a headache. Tiffany had doused several cotton balls with pink acetone to remove the ratty polish from her fingernails. Now Randy was fretting about the odor and the probability of his throwing up. He had a point.

"Tiffany, that's fairly noxious stuff. Do you mind?" Peggy said.

"I'm almost done," she said.

"Mom, make her crack the window at least."

"We're on the interstate," Tiffany said.

"Crack the window, please, Tiffany."

"Finished," she said. Randy rolled down his own window, a sliver of fresh air, and tilted his face toward the whistling stream.

There was nothing for the children to do in the car. Idleness was no friend to any of them. Peggy tried to remember the car games that she and her sisters had played as girls but they seemed archaic to her now. Ceci was content just to be among them, wedged in a small space and snuggling her "night-night." Ceci liked saying every word twice. Sometimes this echo gave a new and larger meaning to the word. Her sweetness was a frequent respite for them and as the little one she required the least of Peggy.

Tiffany said, "I want to live in a yurt."[4]

"What's a yurt?" Randy asked.

Peggy never knew what openings she might have with Tiffany. There were so few, she had to pay close attention. Peggy found the girl (in turn) fascinating, then infuriating. Peggy did not want to hate her daughter. She did not want to lose her or be lost to her. All this was entirely possible. They were talking about yurts now. Peggy offered, "It's sort of a hut."

"No, Mother. It's more of a tent," Tiffany said. "Anyway, you'll probably have to snowshoe in to visit me."

"No thanks!" Randy said.

"Don't worry. You're not even invited to my yurt," Tiffany said. Peggy, apparently, was. Who knew what she had done to deserve an invitation?

Around noon, Peggy tapped at the itinerary sitting in front of her on the dash. "Read this, would you please, Tiffany?"

"One-fifteen p.m.: Stop for lunch."

"Is that all?" Peggy asked.

"No. Mother, this thing is twelve pages long."

Frank's good intentions always went too far. It took years for Peggy to see how exhausting it was, being Frank. After they were married, he had studied her form extensively. There were books

---

4. **yurt** (noun) **yurt** (noun). Also spelled: yourt. [Etymology—Russian yurta (by way of French yourte, perhaps Gernab Jurte) from the Turkic jurt.] A circular tent of animal hides and felted fibers such as wool. Serves as mobile residence for nomadic peoples of Mongolia and Siberia. May also describe a semi-subterranean living space, often constructed of wood and roofed with soil or loam.

about such things, he told her. She suspected Frank had read these books because he became patient and adept. And he did please. But Peggy never could persuade her husband of his prowess, and soon it became all about the convincing instead. Peggy knew if she had told him of this distraction, Frank would have declared the session and her pleasure null. He would have insisted that he begin again (a do-over) and Peggy couldn't bear it. She was already spent and sad.

"Well, why don't you read the rest of dad's itinerary, Fanny?" Randy said. He had chosen his sister's old childish name. He was just a boy, but Randy was trying to step into his father's stead now—to remain loyal to the agenda, as written.

"Read it yourself, you moronic Horny Toad!" Tiffany said. She threw the itinerary at her brother, and Peggy saw her boy smirk. He had outsmarted his sister and had just what he wanted.

"Please," Peggy said. Meaning, please stop. Please be kind to one another. Please! Who was it, Penelope Leach? Dr. Spock? One of them, anyway, had coined a handy acronym for deliberate parenting. H.A.L.T. A wise mother ought to halt if she discerned that her child was Hungry, Angry, Lonely, Tired. The child wouldn't tell, but a good mother ought to simply know her child. Intimately, intuitively. To observe and to know.

"Mother? I was thinking," Tiffany said. This meant the girl wanted something. Peggy listened for what it was. "We don't have to do the trip this way exactly."

"It's all planned," Randy said, "Dad figured it all out so it'll be fun. Smooth sailing, right Mom?" Peggy was sorry. She and Frank were no longer allies. When had this happened? She couldn't say. But they had courted their children, moment by moment, inclining each toward mother or father. They had never spoken of this and it struck Peggy now as subversive and cruel.

"We'll see," Peggy told her son.

At one, Randy said, "How soon until McDonald's?"

"McDonald's is crap," Tiffany said.

"Tiffany," Peggy said.

"What?"

"Just stop." She was asking Tiffany to practice being an adult, just for a little while.

"Fine," Tiffany said. Then, softly to her brother, she hissed, "Mother said Howard Johnson's[5] anyway." The girl thought of herself first (always) and it was ugly. Peggy was on her own. And Randy couldn't help his agenda. It had been assigned to him, really.

"But Dad said McDonald's. On his itinerary."

Tiffany said, "Mother, do they have salad at Howard Johnson's?"

"Donalds! Donalds!" Ceci chanted.

Even the little one had chosen a side. Peggy told her, "Ceci, we want to eat at a nice sit-down place. You watch for the big orange rooftop." Ceci loved the color orange but Peggy spotted it first—right off the highway like she remembered from the annual family trips across the country that she had taken as a girl. "I can hardly believe it. Oh, look! There's the weathervane, too."

Peggy wanted to present the children with something grand. Inside, the dining room was too warm. The blinds were set low against the heat of the day and the restaurant was almost empty. The children were tired and hungry and quiet. After they were settled in their booth Peggy told them, "Now I want you to get a real dinner, not just a burger. This will be our main meal today." Peggy felt for her purse. They could all order whatever they liked. When their meals arrived, Tiffany and Randy dished Ceci nibbles off their plates, turkey with mashed potatoes and thin gravy, pale fish fry dinners.

With some sustenance, Tiffany found her voice again, "This tastes like grandma food. Only bad."

The food was bland. "It's not as good as I remember," Peggy said. "But look, they still have their famous ice cream. And their

---

5. Otherwise known as HoJo's.

big sundae, too, with the special cookie. We always had those when I was a girl."

When the waitress came back, Peggy ordered a sundae for every-one, even Ceci. The waitress said, sorry, the freezer broke last week and melted all the ice cream.

"No ice cream?" Peggy said. For Peggy, it was not the melting ice cream, and missing sundaes, but the lack of ice cream. It was the fact that ice cream was not even an option. This seemed impossibly sad. The waitress looked at Peggy in an odd way and set the check down next to Randy.

Her boy did not know what to do with a check. It was not yet his job to know, so Peggy took it from him, forcing a smile. "I'm sorry about the sundaes. Do you want something else for a treat?"

"That's alright, Mom," Randy told her. "I'm pretty full anyway."

Even Tiffany tried, in the moment, to say what she thought might be the right thing, "Besides, I'm on a diet."

The children bore too much. Peggy knew that this was regret-table, but how to reverse it now? A mother's charge had never seemed fair. It was too much for one woman, even an extraordinary woman. Peggy wasn't sure what she wanted to grieve: these reluctant truths or the missing ice cream.

She asked her little one, "How about you, honey? Do you want another kind of treat? There isn't any ice cream." Ceci was like a sorrow barometer. She took one look at her mother's face and started to cry. "Poor Ceci," Peggy said, holding her. Then it was permissible for Peggy to cry, too, "Mommy is so sorry to disappoint you."

Back in the car, Peggy told them, "By the way, just don't mention to your father that we went to Howard Johnson's."

"Why not?" Randy asked. Howard Johnson's had been a coup, a failed one. So, Randy was testing her loyalty again. Peggy would pull him toward her, likewise.

"Trust me, Randy. Your father does not care for Howard Johnson's."

Hours later, when they reached Flint[6], Peggy was thankful to be landing anywhere. They were all tired of one another and they checked into the hotel Frank had selected for them. Tiffany said she had never seen so many variations of brown and gold and Peggy had to agree. There were two double beds.

Randy asked, "Where will I sleep?"

"Not with me," Tiffany said. She had already set her bag down on the bed closest to the television. The children were exhausted and agitated from confinement and stale air. Peggy sat on the edge of the empty bed.

"Listen," she said, "I am sure we can work something out. There are four places to sleep and there are four of us."

"Five," Randy said.

"What?" Peggy asked

"There are five of us," he said. "One of us isn't here."

He was clever, Randy, and quick. It was an accusation directed at Peggy. She would treat it as an observation.

"That reminds me," she said, "I really should give your father a call."

Ceci was jumping on the bed singing her numbers "One! Two Three! Four! Five!" Randy took care and held onto her little hands as she jumped. Peggy imagined her fickle and valiant boy losing his grip. Her shining uncomplicated girl, jumping too high and sailing into the huge seascape framed on the wall behind her head. A child so small could disappear, like that.

Tiffany chose to occupy her own space. She pulled out a teen magazine and claimed the only chair. Peggy wondered aloud about methods for calling home, "It's probably pretty expensive to use the phone in the hotel room."

"That's okay, Mom," Randy told her. "Dad will want to hear from us." It was not that Peggy begrudged Randy his wish: to speak

---

6. Flint, Michigan: (It used to be really something).

with his father and to report any deviations. She just needed to find Frank's itinerary.

"I think your father said that collect was best. Where's that itinerary?" No one volunteered any thoughts. "Tiffany?"

"How should I know? Randy's the one who had it last," Tiffany said.

"Well, I don't have it," Randy said, but then he scowled. The face he made when he doubted himself. "Maybe I left it in the car. Mom, should I go check?"

"Thank you," Peggy said. (How he wanted to be a good boy.) "I'd appreciate that." Driving into the parking lot that evening in their brand-new car, Peggy had felt not proud or lucky but strangely conspicuous. The car had been the nicest in the lot and she knew how much Randy would relish just being associated with the vehicle.

The television gave Ceci something to do: Julia Child[7] was glazing a roast and sipping her sherry. Ceci found cooking shows hilarious.

"No luck?" Peggy asked Randy when he came back.

"No," he said, and then to Tiffany, "I told you I didn't have it."

Peggy looked at Tiffany, who was thumbing the pages of her magazine. Peggy would have to insist that the girl engage: "Tiffany, can you look through your things, please?"

"In a minute," Tiffany said, still flipping.

"Oh, I'll do it then," Peggy made a show of picking up Tiffany's backpack as if it weighed a ton and Randy laughed. Peggy felt chosen and smiled at her son. She reached into Tiffany's pack. The inner lining was damp. "Tiffany?" she said. Peggy's hand found a clump of wet paper, soaked and heavy, and she pulled it out. The itinerary was stained an irrevocable brown and smelled like a dirty litter box. Near it, an uncapped bottle of Bonne Bell Ten-O-Six Lotion[8].

---

7. Julia Child: 1912–2004; aka The French Chef. Child recalled a transformative meal while in France with her husband in France, reflecting "The whole experience was an opening up of the soul and spirit for me."
8. Bonne Bell Ten-O-Six Lotion, a once popular astringent cleanser for teens, contained urea.

"Tiffany! This itinerary is ruined. I can't even read this anymore." "She did that on purpose!" Randy said. "You did, didn't you?" Tiffany wouldn't look at them, wouldn't even look up from her magazine. "Give me a break," she said. And of course, they were sure now that she had.

"I don't understand this," Peggy said. This girl was subversive, but brazen, too. Peggy almost admired her. It seemed a crucial moment to ask and proclaim the right things but she had no idea what to say to her daughter. "Well?" No. Wait. Establish eye contact. "Tiffany, look at me, please," Peggy said. Tiffany glared at her. It was something.

"Mom, don't worry about the itinerary," Randy said. "I think I remember most of what Dad wrote down."

Peggy thanked her boy, but it was not for his impeccable memory. (She was sorry that he thought he should be the man; that he thought there had to be a man among them.) She was thankful for his effort and for his kindness to her.

Tiffany began stuffing her things into her pack. "This family," she said, "is ludicrous."

Peggy saw that there would be no resolve tonight. Or forgiveness granted. "Why don't you just let everything air out, Tiffany?" she said. Ceci had fallen asleep in a nest of pillows at the foot of the bed. Peggy wanted them all to rest now. But here, Tiffany was pulling her sandals on.

"Oh, no you don't," Peggy said. "It's almost ten. You are not wandering around this hotel alone."

"You know? You're right! I'm dying in here! I'll wander around alone outside instead." Angry, the girl was very angry. And lonely. Her daughter had no company in this circumstance. Peggy would give her some.

"Tiffany. Listen, I understand. I didn't always like that itinerary either. It wasn't my agenda." Tiffany laughed. The girl was heading toward the door.

"Mom!" Randy said. The boy was frightened. This had never happened before. "Tiffany's leaving!"

"I forbid you from leaving this room," Peggy said. At this, she almost laughed herself. Peggy knew that she had only words, and they could not restrain the girl. Tiffany was sixteen, taller than Peggy for years, and strong. Now the girl was out the door.

"Mom!" Randy said.

"I know, I know," Peggy said. She touched her boy's face. "Tiffany will be OK. Your sister's a tough one."

Peggy was not convinced, but she was trying to be convincing. Her boy was awake next to Ceci, listening. Peggy called the police. The woman she spoke with offered only a series of "no's": No, the girl could not be considered a runaway until she was missing twenty-four hours. No, the city's curfew for juveniles wasn't until eleven, so they couldn't pick the girl up until then, if they even found her. No, Peggy should stay there, in the room, so they could call. No, she shouldn't worry. Sometimes these kinds of kids just needed to blow off a little steam. It happened all the time, everywhere, every day.

Waiting, Peggy imagined all the good choices Tiffany would have to make, minute by minute, to bring her safely back. Randy was finally, reluctantly, asleep next to Ceci.

There was no phone call but, well past midnight, three quiet raps and Peggy opened the door for her daughter. A carnival in town, Tiffany said, some cool people, an average party. The girl smelled like pot and beer, nothing too troubling or new. But she let Peggy hold her, wordlessly, for a long time. And Peggy knew that the girl had frightened herself with her own powers and possibility. That night, Peggy lay beside her oldest daughter as she slept. This girl of hers. When had she become so certain and specific? In the dark, Peggy quietly admired the way the girl insisted her clear and rebellious will upon them all.

In the morning, Peggy gassed up the wagon and decided that they needed a nice hot breakfast before returning to the road. She would call Frank, tell him everything, and get her bearings. And they would continue on their way. Randy sat next to Tiffany in the booth at the truck stop restaurant and they both refrained from their usual taunting. The food was surprisingly good: they all said so. Peggy felt a steady, unmedicated calm. She placed a call from the pay-phone, instructed Tiffany and Randy to escort Ceci up and down the aisles of the small store, looking for anything interesting or orange.

"Ready to go?" Peggy asked, after she had finished. They were near the door when Peggy saw the *New York Times* headline: "Health Chief Calls Waste Site a Peril."

"Hold on," she told the children. She picked up the paper and began to read. This couldn't be right.

"What is it?" Tiffany said, leaning over to see, "Oh, that Love Canal[9] thing. I heard about that on the radio earlier, when you were in paying for the gas."

"What Love Canal[10] thing?" Randy asked. "What thing?"

---

9. "Health Chief Calls Waste Site a Peril," (Donald G. McNeil, Jr., the *New York Times*, August 3, 1978. Front Page.)

10. Finding of Fact. Source: State of New York: Department of Health, In the Matter of the Love Canal Chemical Waste Landfill Site Located in the City of Niagara Falls, Niagara County, State of New York, by order of Robert P. Whalen, MD, Commissioner of Health of the State of New York. Date: August 2, 1978

  —The Love Canal is a rectangular, 16-acre, below-ground-level land-fill site located in the southeast corner of the City of Niagara Falls, Niagara County, New York, known as the "La Salle" area, with the southernmost portion of the site about ¼ mile from the Niagara River near Cayuga Island.

  —In the early 19th century the site was excavated as part of a proposed canal project linking the Niagara River and Lake Ontario.

  —The Love Canal project was abandoned and never completed and the abandoned canal subsequently used as a chemical and municipal waste disposal site.

  —The Hooker Chemical Company, Niagara Falls, New York, used the site for the disposal of drummed chemical wastes, process sludges, fly

Peggy was trying to read, listen to Randy's questions, but she had to think. She led her children to a red bench near a display of maps and sat them down. Ceci was turning a small flashlight on and off, pressing the point against her finger to make it glow. Peggy told them, "Listen, this is really a mess. And it's in Niagara Falls. Where we were headed."

"What do you mean, *were* headed?" Randy said.

"Let me see that," Tiffany said, reading the paper over Peggy's shoulder.

Randy pressed, "Mom, you mean *are* headed, right? Where we *are* headed."

"Please, Randy. I'm trying to think."

Tiffany looked up from the paper and said, "Well, big surprise there. Another man-made wasteland."

What Peggy should have felt (was sure any good mother would feel) was outrage followed swiftly by compassion. Because life wasn't meant to be this way. These were people's homes[11]. Families lived

---

ash, and other wastes, for a period of nearly 25 years, from on or about 1930 to on or about 1953.

—The City of Niagara Falls, New York, also used the site for the disposal of municipal wastes for many years prior to and including 1953.

—On or about 1953, the site was covered with earth and sold by the Hooker Chemical Company to the Board of Education of the City of Niagara Falls, New York.

—The City of Niagara Falls Board of Education subsequently sold part of the site to others.

11. Finding of Fact, Continued.

—There are presently 97 families with 230 adults and 134 children living in the houses adjacent to the northern and southern sections of the Love Canal.

—The basements of homes bordering the site are now suffering from toxic chemical waste leachate intrusion from the site.

—The grammar school has no basement, but a crawl space only, however the possibility of standing water next to the classroom windows provides a mechanism for the transportation of and exposure of the school children to toxic vapors.

there: mothers and fathers and children. Instead, Peggy felt only uncertainty as to how to proceed. Tiffany had a new enthusiasm.

"I wonder if we'll get to see a protest or something!"

"We're not still going," Peggy said, but that thought had just come. "This is pretty bad. The Health Commissioner of New York State is calling this 'a situation of great and imminent peril.' That is not my idea of a family vacation." Peggy's thoughts were coalescing now. "And I can't knowingly put the three of you in harm's way."

"But dad's itinerary!" Randy said. "We can't just turn around. Please, Mom. Check with Dad. Check with Triple A!" Peggy understood her boy, how earnest he was, and how certain that they should keep on.

"Oh, this figures," Tiffany said. "Just when this trip is finally getting interesting, we bail."

The threat was in the city of Niagara Falls. In a residential community. Contained, it seemed, to a site called the La Salle area. As their mother, Peggy was responsible for getting their lunch, arranging their vaccinations, folding their clean clothes, and maintaining their innocence. At times she was resolved and at others simply undone. A mother had to pay such vigilant attention.

If a woman were permitted to be both, in this moment, Peggy was a bad person and a good mother. She didn't care about the Love Canal or the people who shouldn't be there. She was thinking of her children. She was thinking of their beginnings and their endings, of their whole lives, and her own. She would keep the radio on for the rest of the drive to Niagara Falls, just in case there was anything new to learn. There were so many possibilities, it seemed. And countless ways to save your children.

WHAT WE TELL OURSELVES

We smile at the Polish immigrant girl packing up our reusable grocery bags. In goes the multi-grain waffle mix, organic raspberries, and local raw honey.

We watch the way the girl's thin hands, her elegant bony (foreign) hands, move with an efficiency that we suspect has been locked into her genomic sequence out of necessity. Maybe a dozen free-range eggs and a nice pork loin.

One day, we know, the Polish girl will have a family of her own to feed. But hopefully not anytime too soon, because we all know that she would be better off getting some kind of degree or licensure, going at least to community college. French Roast coffee beans to grind fresh back at the lake house in the morning. Perhaps dental hygiene if she has a fondness for sharp things! Hold on. Throw in these breath mints. But one day, when her hips are ready, we are certain, the Polish girl's children's hands, and her children's children's hands, and so on, will move likewise. We look at our own hands, and give the Polish immigrant girl our AmEx card.

Down the road, at Ye Olde Fudge Shoppe, we exchange cash with the pock-faced local boy for cones of sweet—glacial!—cream that shock our straight white teeth. Full regimes of orthodontia, all.

We are the summer people. But don't conflate us—please!—with those East Coast old-money types who head off to the Hamptons. Or wherever. We've all seen that in the movies. We are the *Midwestern* summer people. In June, we migrate to the lake house with our collections of gifted children and stay as long as we can. The loamy soil gives a little under our comfortable new sandals. The spring fed lake welcomes us back, another year's worth of curated triumphs and secret regrets.

Our blue screens glow on the screen porch at night. Even at the lake house, we like our Wi-Fi and Netflix. We don't apologize. This is who we are. At JJ's coffee shop, we take our conference calls from work if we need to. It's all part of doing business. We drop a five in JJ's tip jar—"for counter intelligence"—and grin at the word play. If the townies hate us, they like our money well enough. We are supporting the local economy. Hell, we *are* the local economy.

We humor the old bachelor who inherited a little cabin on the lake from his grandfather. Everybody knows Crazy Al. He's harmless, we say, just an eccentric. Lonely, and broke, and lucky to even have that ratty little place. We do not consider the disrepair charming. But we do remember someone telling us once that Crazy Al wasn't always this way. He had suffered some kind of traumatic brain injury. Maybe in a war? Or a car accident? Something. Now, Crazy Al rides an old Schwinn bicycle and forgets to wear his pants sometimes. And he won't let us pass by his property without offering us a gift: a wind-mobile he has fashioned out of soda cans. In his swept-dirt yard we bet he's got at least twenty of those things hanging from the pine trees. Thin strips of aluminum fan-out into flowers, peacocks, and sunbursts, each one spinning into a blur of unabashed color and symmetry. When the air is still, though, they shout out words like "Grape!!" and "Diet Cola!!!" Really, they are nothing more than shredded generic pop cans stuck on bent coat hangers. We know this display is an eyesore. We've complained here and there. But Crazy Al's family has been on the lake for generations. That's got to be worth something, right?

We like abundance, and we have it. We come prepared with lots of bug sprays and creams, some natural and some napalm. None of us want Lyme disease! We stock our pine cupboards with jumbo packs of toilet paper so we never run out. Of course, we keep the liquor cupboard well appointed, high and low, and the second refrigerator full of craft beer or electrolyte enhanced water.

We do want a nice tan for our white Midwestern skin, something to show for our time at the lake, but we don't want skin cancer or wrinkles. We have sun blocks, and sunscreens, and sun hats, and sun glasses, and sun shirts. We remember that one time in Cabo when we got so burned we literally could not move. God, we felt like we were literally going to die! But now that we think about it, we really do not want pain of any kind. So there are pills, too. Most any kind we like. But that's private. We think that a lot of things are private, and not really topics we find appropriate at the lake house, including depression, anxiety, impending job loss, recent miscarriages, sus-pected/denied/confirmed infidelity, and high functioning alcohol-ism. Correction! We do not mind, and rather enjoy, talking about the depression, anxiety, impending job loss, recent miscarriages, suspected/denied/confirmed infidelity, and high functioning alco-holism that we have observed or suspect involving other people.

We drink cocktails on the pontoon boat and cruise the lake, watching for eagles, and families of loons. When the townies rent jet-skis and put in at the public dock after work or on weekends, we do not appreciate the noise. We teach our children to catch and release, how to let the minnows bite their chubby white toes, how to water ski, how to shake hands, how to make pancakes. We don't teach our children how to scrub a toilet, because even here at the lake house, we hire that out. Because, really, we are here to relax, to summer, not to clean. Instead, we feed eager hummingbirds sugar water that we bring to a boil, cool on the kitchen counter, and fun-nel into artisan blown-glass feeders that we admire when the low sun hits them, just so.

When we gather at our annual Lake Association meeting, we worry about the townies putting their boats in at the public dock on our lake. On weekends, there they are with their pick-ups and rusty trailers. We are sure they haven't read the newest literature on Eurasian Milfoil and Zebra Mussels from the DNR. Do they really understand the dangers of invasive species?

Back at the lake house, the nights are getting cooler. In our yard, we don't notice that a few birch trees have fallen and are starting to rot. One of us tells a funny story about Crazy Al, and we laugh. We like Crazy Al well enough. It's not that. Actually, we just really don't like the way that Crazy Al *looks* at us sometimes. When we are out on walk, we prefer not to linger too long when Crazy Al just appears near the road. Where does he come from? It's unnerving, we say. So, even though we know that Crazy Al is no threat to us—we're not the crazy ones here!—we do move along quickly. As politely as we can, we quickly move away from Crazy Al, we exit the almost imperceptible *Zzzzzzzzzt* of his peculiar energy field. We move as though—if we were to stay a moment longer—we might catch his scarcity, his loss.

THE GHOST OF L.T. BOWSER TELLS WHAT REALLY WENT DOWN

To set the record straight, my trouble with Mr. O_____ began shortly after I came to Minneapolis under the employ of the General Chemical Company. But it was no fault of my own. If Mr. O_____ were here today, instead of likely rotting in Hell, I imagine that he would confess his blame. Simply put, the man didn't like me.

Hazel was determined to make a go of it here. It was January, 1931. She had to take in sewing and raise my dead wife's boys. How could she not resent me? (But the truth always comes out: she divorced me thirty-one years later. There you have it!)

Here in the warehouse, I went about my work as well as any man could manage. And when I made certain the ammonia and sulfuric acid were finally housed in proper drums, when I built and balanced an accurate scale, when I kept the new operation running along, as best I could, despite the cold, despite the poor lighting, despite the quarrelsome soap swindlers next door, would it have pained my superior, Mr. Sword, to say to me: nice work? But, no. I don't hold a grudge. Mr. Sword knew the truth. I kept him abreast of our progress, (as well as my disagreements with the very disagreeable Mr. O_____), in my frequent letters to New York.

Oddly, all the men under me in the warehouse were hard to get on with. My dead wife Elizabeth would have told me that some people are just born difficult. One must have compassion for them.

And of dying the way she did, a young mother, leaving me so soon? She would have said that the Lord took her in His timing. No, the only providence there was that Elizabeth never saw what I became: a mere worker, indexing and storing and shipping. What? Chemicals I didn't discover, acids I didn't formulate. Shuttling barrels of caustic poison from here to there, here to there, for another man's profit and another man's purpose? Ha!

Hazel would scold me whenever I complained: "You have work. Be thankful! So, you didn't become a great man? No one ever does." She had a point.

And though I imagine my Elizabeth, too, would have endured, I am glad death spared her from such a compromised life.

Funny. I like to linger here now. This place is more than it once was, yet everything remains. It is a curious thing. I have just begun to notice how often the low winter sun shines brightly, even when the wind is cruel.

TELL THE SWEDE I'M GAME

I was still a little kid and Betty was still a drunk when a boy showed up in our driveway early one morning with a black eye and dirty underwear. That was Titus. We brought him inside and he pretty much stayed. Sometimes Titus went home to sleep, but no one in his house asked any questions the nights he didn't, and that's just plain wrong. When Betty was in her cup and looking for something to do, she would boost Titus up onto the kitchen counter near the sink. He just sat there, her little stooge, and let her decorate him with blue eye shadow, lip gloss, whatever she wanted, all over his face. I guess he loved her like a mother.

Fast-forward twenty years, and Betty sobered up. I'm convinced that she skipped a step, because she got all over me about my shit. Key word: my shit. Even Titus and I knew that. I had tried to let Betty off the hook when she first made her amends to me, but I was still at the top of her list and she was ready to lay down the cash to make things better. The problem was Betty seemed to be developing a series of progressively unreasonable aspirations for me ever since she got dry. I was smart, she kept saying. But I already knew that. We met at the chichi breakfast place near my building. Betty would pay my way with her dead father's money, like she always did. Because of him, neither of us had to work. Betty said all of that money had pushed her out of her league. I was used to living like this, and thought the money came in handy. But she had liked her league,

Betty would say. Her hair was dyed a brutal red to prove that she was still a wild card. When my eggs came, Betty started in on me.

She wanted me to know that she held herself accountable for what I have become. My issues were no new revelation. I could recite the whole drill. My belongings are not me. They are a burden and a distraction. So says the Doc, when the clock is ticking. Titus calls me a packrat. He means it with affection. My ex-girlfriend called me pathological and then I called her a Spartan bitch and that was that. Betty explained that it wasn't really my fault that I was such a loser. That was supposed to make me feel better.

"Thanks, Betty," I said. She got quiet. "I'm just kidding." I told her. I can usually say whatever I want, as long as I claim that I'm only joking.

"Oh!" Betty said, and smiled at me.

She wanted to buy me a professional organizer from Sweden. The Swede's name was Brigitte. I told Betty that I didn't have a problem with that.

"Perfect," Betty said, "just perfect."

"How long do I get to keep her?" I said. It took Betty a beat.

"This is her work, Kenny," Betty told me. She sounded tired.

"Fine," I said, "How old is she?" I was serious about that. I didn't want some foreign grandma going through my personal possessions.

"Kenny, don't you start thinking things." This was Betty's latest euphemism for s-e-x.

"I don't want to nail her," I said, but then I actually kind of did. "Really, how old is she, anyway?" I imagined a Swedish ski bunny and that did the trick. But then I thought I was a pretty sick bastard for deliberately raising the flag while I was talking to my mother. The Doc would call that an Invasive Thought. I would ask him, which thought? And even though I would be seeking genuine clarification, he wouldn't answer my question because he'd think I had attempted a joke. The Doc wanted me to take myself seriously.

"I honestly couldn't say her age. Thirty-something, I guess," Betty said.

Thirty sounded good enough, but I didn't like being Betty's only pastime. With no substances to buy now (save coffee and cigarettes; you can't be expected to give up everything that feels good, so coffee and cigarettes were encouraged in recovery), Betty had even more spare change to fix me with. Even though I have to give Betty props for how long she'd been dry, the jury's still out for me on the issue of abstinence. When you think about it, what kind of courage does it take to lock your favorite demon in a cage? A baby started socializing like a siren in a corner booth. I looked down at my eggs, but I couldn't make sense of anything with all the noise.

Betty raised her voice over the baby, "What about Thursday morning? Tomorrow. Brigitte says she has to come two days in a row, so you'll have to keep Friday open, too."

I was thinking a new hobby would be good for Betty. Maybe scrapping, because that was a verb now. I had seen a large southern woman selling a pink and black suitcase full of photo album paraphernalia late at night on the Home Shopping Network. Like seven out of ten American women, Betty still had a box full of memorabilia. I was in there, and usually Titus was, too, gathering dust and decomposing under the guest bed. I didn't like the pictures Betty had taken on vacations when she was still a drunk, but they told the story. I remember how pissed Betty would get after she picked up the prints. There we were, supposedly living it up at a Wisconsin water park where the beer flowed like a lazy river, so why in the hell did we look so miserable? I have to admit, it was a lot easier doing Betty's bidding when she was still drunk. The duties were pretty basic: pick up, mop up, shut up. Now she was being righteous and I didn't have the heart to deny her that. Plus, I always got this peculiar little rush letting her think she was doing me a favor, when I was the one doing the giving.

Betty knew I had nowhere I had to be on Thursdays. "Tell the Swede I'm game."

I called Titus at the motel where he was living. Titus lived like a dirtbag, and he wouldn't take any money from Betty. I couldn't tell if this was some ethical code he'd learned on television or if he was being proud. Once in a while he let Betty give him a gift card to a grocery store or gas station. He'd make her happy by taking the card and making it last. I told Titus about the Swede that Betty had ordered up and he offered to help me clear a path to my bed, just in case.

I hadn't had a woman in my apartment for two years, ever since my last real girlfriend. I got plenty, though. I went to her place, whoever she was. I was a charmer when I stayed the whole night and made scrambled eggs in the morning. I let all the women think whatever they needed to think. That is what you call a win-win situation.

Titus asked, "So, is the Swede hot?"

I decided to take the high road. Most days, Titus gave me the leverage and I liked that about him. "Who knows?" I said. But she was. I had already checked out her website. The black and white headshot didn't fool me, her symmetrical teeth and intelligent nose. She was so pretty. I had already forgiven her for being pretentious.

I told him, "This is self-improvement shit, Titus. Get it? Besides, we're really doing this for Betty. Are you in?" Titus had taken care of Betty almost as much as me.

"I'm in," he said. I imagined or heard a tinny rattle, him thinking about it some more, "Maybe I should bring my truck."

"Very funny," I said.

Titus showed up at my door with a mop and a bucket.

"What the hell is that?" I said. I was pissed off, but not at him. I didn't care. We were used to this. It was how we did things.

"We're cleaning up, right?" he said. In truth, Titus's brain had some serious divots from all the substances we had done together when we were young. We had slowed down pretty significantly over the last few years, but I guess I was the lucky one, cerebrally speaking.

From the outset, Titus didn't have as much gray matter to squander, so you had to have compassion for the lack.

"Set that shit down, will you? We're just moving my stuff out of the way." We stood together and really looked around. It was pretty bad.

"I kind of lost track," Titus said, "You have a shit load of shit, Kenny, you know that?"

"I know," I said. I felt alone right then, even with Titus standing there next to me.

Then Titus pulled a quintessential Titus. "No problem," he said. That was Titus in true form. Titus incarnate. One thing I knew, I could count on Titus. "We should start in the kitchen. That's where we should start." Titus was granting himself authority for once, and I was relieved. "Let's toss those pizza boxes, Kenny."

I explained that I was saving the pizza boxes as a method of record keeping for budgeting purposes. He didn't get it. It was kind of complicated. If I always ordered a medium from Rosetta's then the boxes were the same size and they folded mostly flat. Thirty boxes roughly equaled a month of dinners. Recently, I had started stacking them sideways. Except I didn't like how any of this sounded out loud.

Titus looked around the kitchen. The mail had gotten out of hand. I could see that. I told him how I was waiting for the right time to read everything, chronologically. There were probably one hundred stupid things Titus could have said at that moment, and Titus possessed no shortage of stupid, but he said, "So, what's off limits?"

I was glad to have his perspective on the task before us, and his approach made perfect sense to me. We decided to make labels. I found a piece of paper and roll of masking tape in my money drawer. Titus went and got a Bic from the glove box in his truck. He folded and creased and tore the paper into strips. There were twenty-two strips of paper. Titus gave me a smile. He knew about my thing for even numbers.

He said, "Is that enough?"

I looked around. I didn't think so. We worked together and tore the strips in half, so now we had forty-four strips of paper, each the size of my pinky finger.

I also put Titus in charge of writing the labels, because he had amazing penmanship for someone who got such shitty grades in school. I told him so and he said thanks. I wasn't the first to recognize this skill.

"Let's write OFF LIMITS in capital letters," he said.

I thought about the pretty Swede walking into my place the next day, all the things she might already hold against me. I didn't want to be rude on top of everything else.

"Wait," I told him, "better make that PLEASE LEAVE." Linguistically the connotation was a request instead of a command, and who doesn't prefer to be asked instead of told?

When Titus was finished, I put the first PLEASE LEAVE on one of the pizza boxes.

"Better make sure the Swede knows you mean all of them," Titus said. He had a good point.

"Right," I said. I was so thankful for his leadership in this situation. I was going to have to tell the Doc about this on Monday. The Doc wanted me to relinquish some control and he would call this progress. I had learned to throw the Doc a bone once in a while. After all this time, he could get pretty discouraged with me.

"What's next?" Titus asked. He was looking at my video-disc collection. In my opinion, there is a lot of crap calling itself entertainment these days. I had watched hundreds of sadistic reality shows where family members ambushed one another in the name of love. The double agent always had some unresolved issue with her fat sister's underarm odor or her husband's closet full of baseball caps. It even made me a little sad for the hoarders, for all of them. But no one was touching my video-disc collection.

"These have to stay," I told Titus, taping a PLEASE LEAVE on some episodes of *The Walking Dead*.

"Which ones?" Titus said.

"All of them," I said, but I saw his doubt. I looked again. My collection took up most of the north wall.

"Even the blank ones?" Titus asked. Those discs weren't actually blank, but I understood the mistake.

"I need those, too," I explained. "I just haven't labeled them yet."

"Oh," Titus said, "You know, maybe you should write this stuff down. For the Swede."

"We don't have time for that," I said. There were too many systems at work in my apartment to explain it all to someone like Titus. He opened my refrigerator door.

"Old Milwaukee?" he said, handing me a bottle. Sometimes Titus knew what I needed most in the world. We still drank Old Mil after all these years. That's what we had started with when we were eleven. Popping one was like coming home.

"My man," I said, taking it.

He took the last one for himself, and I gave him a nod. We sat down on the floor to assess the situation. We got to talking about other things.

"Remember that vampire girl you were with for a while?" I said, "What ever happened to her?" That girl was a complete whack job but Titus's bedroom report had been visceral.

"Who?" he said.

"The vampire girl. You know, you met her at Mac's? Don't be a dick." I thought he was bragging, as if a girl like her was nothing to a man like him.

He said, "Oh, right. I don't know what her story is."

I could see now that he honestly didn't remember her and I felt like the dick. Titus really got to me sometimes. He finished the rest of his beer. "Break's over," he said.

My right hand was a fist full of PLEASE LEAVES and Titus was getting bossy. I wasn't used to working this hard. "Maybe we should head over there," I said.

"To Mac's?" Titus asked. I was impressed that he had been following that thread of the conversation pretty well. I told him we had gotten a lot done and it seemed like an appropriate way to celebrate.

"Kenny, this place is still full of shit."

Titus was on to me. And he was right, I knew it. Titus was a true friend, but I wanted to get the hell out of there and about now he'd be needing another beer. Bitter like an aspirin on my tongue, I gave him back his beautiful words:

"No problem," I said, "We'll just hit Mac's for a few. Don't worry, man. We'll come back here and finish all this before the Swede shows up."

Titus let me take care of the tab most nights. We'd had a few and Titus was getting comfortable and I was glad to be anywhere but my apartment. Some old chick I'd never seen before kept feeding quarters into Mac's jukebox and singing "Love Me Tender" along with Elvis, over and over again. She was awful.

"God, she sucks," I said to Titus.

"Who cares?" he said.

"I'm trying to relax, and Ms. Presley here is not helping." I watched her sway. You could tell she was pretty bad off.

"Anyway, we should get back to your place," Titus said. He hadn't forgotten.

"Well, I've had about enough of that serenade," I said to Titus. I stood up. Titus did too. He thought we were leaving. But I told him, "Just a minute. I need to have a word with the entertainment."

"Kenny, come on," Titus said. He didn't know what I was up to, and I wasn't sure yet either.

"You like that song, huh?" I said to her.

"Hey! It's you!" she said. Ms. Presley came toward me then, all familiar, her arms reaching out to hug me. She thought I was somebody, and she was breathing her stink into my face. Up close she looked even worse.

"Oh no. No thanks. We'll have none of that," I held my arm out to block her, but it came off like a little shove.

"Kenny," Titus said, "take it easy."

Ms. Presley tried smiling at me, but her eyes were half-mast and her jowls were hanging slack from all the booze.

"Sweetheart," she said. God, she disgusted me! "Baby, don't you know me?"

She starting coming at me again. What did she want?

"Look at yourself, why don't you?" She was lurching toward me, and I pushed her away, hard this time. Down she went. "You're such a mess."

I wanted to exchange a knowing glance with Titus, one that said we agreed about Ms. Presley, but Titus was staring at me like I was the stranger.

A man about my age came over.

"Hey, take it easy, man," he said, putting his arm around her, pulling her up. "She's with me. She thinks you're somebody else." Even now, Ms. Presley was blowing me kisses. "Time to go, Liz," the man was steering her toward the door, "you've got the wrong guy."

Titus was already sitting back down, his hangdog-head hanging down over what was left of his beer. I knew that stance. I knew that he was mad at me, and I ordered us another round.

"That wasn't very nice," he told me, "she didn't know which end was up."

"I didn't hurt her," I said, "Anyway, who cares? She's just a drunk. She won't remember a thing."

But Titus wasn't finished with me yet, "You know better, Kenny. She didn't do anything to you. And you know what, Kenny? You can be a real asshole. You could afford to be a lot nicer."

I told Titus he had an excellent point. I couldn't argue with that. Titus had come to help me with my shit and he had come because of Betty. That part was the same old story: I was an asshole, and a packrat, and a loser with some money.

But here was something new. After this beer? I was done being Betty's counterfeit redemption.

Sitting at Mac's with Titus beside me, I conjured a pleasing image of the Swede. How beautiful she looked as she prepared to start the day. How the morning sun would brush her fair shoulders, while she stood outside my apartment door, waiting for me.

WALTER BOMBARDIER TELLS A BIG FAT LIE

At sixty-eight, Walter Bombardier was troubled by any muddling of old and new. He did not have cable television or an email account. Walter Bombardier collected rare books, and between his mattress and matching box spring, kept a leather date book in which he recorded every precious acquisition. Delaney was his favorite dealer and theirs was a symbiotic relationship. Although it was becoming commonplace now (and hats off to William Shockley for his Nobel Prize and what not), still, Walter was distressed at the notion of trading in books through what amounted to a cipher of binary code housed in a box full of micro-transistors. It seemed nearly sacrilege, like a well-meaning but pungent youngster with an acoustic guitar strumming away in a cathedral.

Walter's dealer had a website now. A virtual store, they called it. (Oh, Delaney, Delaney.) And for once, Walter Bombardier had a legitimate reason to be pissed off. A whole new level of pissed off. It was no mistake that Walter, being a brisk walker still, could arrive at Delaney's store front in less than seven minutes. But Walter's proximity? It meant nothing when some other man bought the 1909 copy of Malory's *Le Morte* that Walter had all but spoken for. And now, thwarted, Walter could think of nothing other than this other man (with his betrothed!) opening and touching what should have rightly belonged to him. This other man, with what? An American Express Card? A laptop computer? Internet capability?

That morning in his date book Walter Bombardier wrote: "Bit-head enfant snags my vintage Le Morte. Delaney turncoat. Situation unacceptable." Walter then telephoned Delaney to admonish him.

"What's this? Oh, Bombardier. It's just you," Delaney said, "Listen, it was an all-out bidding war, I kid you not. This was way out of your league." Out of his league? Delaney had no idea of Walter's reserves.

"I thought we had an understanding," Walter said. He had wanted that book, Delaney knew it, "but apparently you are not a man of your word."

"Oh, please, don't forget how long I've done business with you."

Walter, had he been Delaney, would have chosen more familiar words to refer to what they had shared for almost twenty-five years. He would have begun: "Come now, Walter," and closed, warmly, by saying, "Let's not forget how long we've been friends," or at the very least "how long we have known one another." Delaney went on, though, in his own fashion.

"You cool off. And be sure to give me a call next week, before I leave for the Chicago auction." Walter would do no such thing. There was no going back. He had banished others from his life for far lesser offenses.

That night, Walter began unwittingly traveling to cyberspace in his dreams. Here he played the role of a naked astronaut with malfunctioning oxygen equipment. These dreams did not end well, but their disquiet was of great use to Walter, as nightly (unbeknownst to him) new and unexpected corridors opened in his mind, and thus he began to contemplate the possibility of trading online, and the potential, oh! the potential! Until, by day, words and wires also began firing and fusing, taking hold of Walter's head like an unin-vited, yet reliable, fantasy.

These visions decided it: Walter succumbed to the call. He would join the masses in their Internet Age, but Walter had no idea how to proceed. He knew that he needed a cup of black coffee, some basic information, a place to sit down. Every morning he walked to Mick's

Place (where the booths were still real leather and the tables were made of hard wood) for a cup of coffee. So today ought not to be an exception. At Mick's, Walter was used to his brief exchange with the regular girl, and he did not recognize the one standing there now. She was sprite of a woman (no, a girl) with the name "Jennie" pinned like a brooch at her neck. She wore green reading glasses and a silver stud through her tongue. Walter ordered a small dark roast from her.

"And pardon me, Miss," Walter said.

"What? Do you want something from the bakery, too?" the girl asked, setting Walter's coffee down on the counter between them.

"No," he said, but revised mid-sentence. He would retrain his tongue toward a mild civility, "Thank you, no. I wanted to ask about those newspapers." She tilted her head like a house wren (a question) so Walter indicated the metal rack of newspapers near the door with a throw of his hand.

"Oh, those are the local freebies. Help yourself."

"Yes, thank you. I wanted to ask your opinion though, which do you think might appeal to a computer savvy sort of person?"

The girl came out from behind the counter (small, elfish) and pulled three different papers from the rack, placing them side-by-side on a table for two. She instructed Walter, tapping each paper as she went.

"Let's see, we've got *Girlz Timz*. Total crap by the way. And *Job Hunt*. Ha! I'm sure those are *real* winners! Then, we have *Net News*," she patted Walter's arm, "that's the one you want, OK?" Her work done, she left Walter there with his papers and coffee.

Walter sat down. He would take the girl's swift assistance, even her presence at Mick's today, as a sign of his good fortune. Then he remembered his manners and called out to her, "Thank you," squinting to get her name on her neck again, "Jennie." She looked so pleased! (Why, she even laughed!)

"Sophie is my real name," she told him, "I just wear this nametag to fool the powers that be." She whispered now, though it was just the two of them, "It's sort of a self-preservation exercise."

"Well, thank you then, Sophie," he said.

"You are most welcome—" She was waiting. For his name. It had been many years since Walter had felt anything like this, this barely discernable hum, this low-voltage of energy that, unbidden, could link one with another. But, oh, he felt it now.

"Walter," he told her.

"Then you are most welcome, *Walter*," she said. And with that, she went into the back, taking the current with her.

Walter looked down at the newspaper Sophie had placed before him. He had lost all focus. What exactly was he looking for? He supposed a consultant. For a reasonable fee. The consultant would need to be willing to come to Walter's apartment. And not charge for mileage. Walter turned to the classified section of *Net News*. There were many, many institutions offering coursework in computer repair and promising decent steady employment. A non-profit organization called "Computers for a Cause" would gladly take Walter's used hardware to be refurbished for non-descript but noble purposes. Sophie appeared behind him, pressing the edge of her blouse and beneath that her slim hip against his arm. The sharpness of her surprised and pleased him. She leaned over, reading along with Walter. He waited for her to say something and when she did not, felt aroused and then obliged by her nearness.

"Nothing yet, I'm afraid," he said.

"What is it you want anyway?" she asked, tilting again. At this moment, what he wanted most was to be clever for her. He thought to say: to buy my very own bit-head! Ha! But with no context, the humor might be lost on the girl and he would seem a fool.

"Well?" she said, and laughed at his brief pause. (How quickly she seemed to move!) "Do you even know what it is you want?" Walter felt the sting of the question's accurate mark, but chose to stand firm in his resolve toward a new and deliberate kindness.

Now Sophie sat down opposite Walter at the table. He was becoming quite taken with her. The realization came when she met his gaze: it had been over 15 years since he had dined with a pretty girl. And he had never dined with, had never encountered, really, a girl like Sophie. "I need a consultant," he told her, "a hired gun, if you will."

She was not tilting her head this time. He would try for a joke now, "To attempt to drag me kicking and screaming into the Age of the Internet."

She smiled at him, now. "Is that all? Well today must be your lucky-lucky day, Walter! I can totally hook you up."

"You can?" Walter was struck by a lovely image of this girl, Sophie, in his apartment, bending over to plug something in. She patted Walter's thin forearm again with her warm hand.

"Absolutely. I'm exactly what you need."

Sophie wrote her cell phone number down on the back of a punch card intended for loyal coffee drinkers to track the frequency of their consumption. Walter didn't know anything about this girl. He needed her to be qualified. He ought to inquire about her training and experience. She was, after all, just a coffee shop girl. But she was already moving ahead without him.

"Don't worry, Walter. I'm kind of a freelancer." He was to call her first thing tomorrow. There was really no time to waste.

At seven the next morning, Walter awoke to an exuberant knocking on his door. He opened it, and there stood Sophie, her arms full with a nest of cables and wires. Her bare stomach peered at him between the small t-shirt and blue jeans she wore. An intricate tattoo, a ring of thorns, circled her navel. He looked up to her face: the plastic glasses were gone, her eyes were bright green, several gnarled pigtails perched at the top of her head. Walter was so glad to see her, but he had not been expecting her. He could not recall telling Sophie where he lived. Yet, he must have, for here she was.

"Well, good morning," he said, "I can see that you mean business."

"Yes, and I can see that I have woken you up," Sophie said. She set her things down on Walter's dining room table where he kept his aging personal computer and stacked his papers. Her arms free now, she faced him, reached out and placed her hands on each of his shoulders. Sophie greeted him with a quick kiss in the air next to each cheek. "Here I am!" she said.

"Thank you for coming," Walter said.

Sophie produced an actual scroll of parchment, and handed it to Walter.

"Presentation," she told him. It was splendid.

"Of course," Walter said, unrolling. It was a list, written with a nib in real ink by an experienced calligrapher's hand.

"Read it out loud," Sophie said, "I can't wait to hear your voice." It was an odd request, an odd way to request it, but he would gladly do as she asked. Now Sophie was closing her eyes.

Walter tried his best to resonate for her, "Project Walter," that was him, "One, Provider decisions. Two, Establish connection. Three, Navigation lesson. Four, Communication 101. Five, Solo flight." He hoped that he had read it well.

"Very nice," Sophie said, "I dreamed that whole thing up last night. Isn't it just poetry? And it's also my official proposal. Should you accept, it would take us about three days, give or take. But we really have to get started right away, Walter. I'm pretty booked out next month. What do you think?"

Walter was still trying to catch up with her. Sophie made him feel terribly rushed and oddly cared for. He tried to recall if they had spoken of her hourly rate. He didn't even know if he could afford her. He should have asked her about this back at the coffee shop.

"This looks very fine," he rolled the parchment, tried handing it back to her. She wouldn't take it, "I'm sorry, though, could you please remind me about your fee?"

She was moving toward his bookshelves, "I see that you're quite a collector."

He was on guard now, "That's right."

"Impressive," she was still looking, but not touching his books. Sophie knew enough not to touch. Walter could learn to respect a girl who knew such things.

"Thank you," Walter said, "and your fee?"

"Oh, right. That's pretty important to you, I see," she turned toward him. "You decide."

"I decide?"

"Yes. After we are done. You assess the value of services rendered, and you pay me. Cash." He did not understand.

"Don't worry," she said, "it always works out. Say, do you have any grapefruit juice?"

"No," Walter said. She flitted, this girl, "I'm afraid not. Listen, I'd like some notion of what this is going to cost me, a range at least, before we go on."

"Walter, please. This is the way. Whatever you deem as fair, as I said. Trust me, it works out beautifully. Everyone leaves completely happy. How about some tomato juice, then?"

Walter doubted the tomato juice, but he couldn't clear his mind about the rest. Regardless, he needed a moment to gather himself, "I'll go and check in the kitchen for that juice."

"With salt," she said.

He was to decide her fee. Who had ever heard of such a thing? Walter was amazed to find an unopened and unexpired bottle of Bloody Mary mix waiting for him in his own cupboard. He hoped that it would do for Sophie. Walter began to rinse out the coffee mug that he used every day for everything but coffee, and then stopped himself. He reached up to the top shelf for a glass, rinsed the dust away, and poured the serendipitous drink for Sophie. Walter returned to her in the living room.

"Thank you," she said. Sophie took one sip, frowned, and handed the glass back to Walter. He was ashamed to be disappointing her so soon.

"It's Bloody Mary mix. I'm afraid it's the closest thing I had to what you wanted."

"Oh, that's not it," she said, "you just forgot the salt."

Now even her palate was beginning to fascinate him. The mix was surely a cacophony of spices, yet she had detected the missing salt. Walter felt convicted, lacking. Back in the kitchen, he gave the glass three shakes for good measure.

"Here you are," he said.

She smiled at Walter, and tasted, "That's better." Her approval buoyed him so.

Sophie sat down on Walter's sofa and placed her hand on the cushion beside her, "Please, join me." Walter sat. "Now," she faced him, "what have you decided?"

"About your fee?" he said. He had thought six hundred, maybe eight, at the most.

She laughed again. How easily she laughed, and with such a brightness behind it. How he wished to make her laugh like that, but never to be the cause of it. Sophie must have seen some semblance of this thought cross Walter's brow. (How remarkable!)

She said to him, softly, "Listen, do you want my help? That's all I meant. Have you decided that you want me to help you?"

Walter told her yes, he was quite certain that he did want that.

By nine that morning, Sophie's friend Michael from the cable company was happy to put a rush on broadband hookup in Walter's apartment. For Sophie, Walter had walked to the market twice, once for grapefruit juice and then again for jalapeño-stuffed green olives. Nearly every fifteen minutes, Sophie's cell phone played a rousing pop tune, which Walter couldn't name. She answered every time and attended to the caller, yet her quick hands never stopped doing their work on Walter's behalf. Her end of each conversation was effusive and succinct, "Hello! Yes! Sounds wonderful! What time? Great! Call me!" she would say to them all.

Benjamin arrived at ten. He was another friend of Sophie's, also from the cable company, who installed Walter's hookup (no charge!) before completing his two previously scheduled jobs in the neighborhood. Walter had completed what he could of his daily crossword

puzzle and had made a modest pretense of dusting several bookshelves. (The cleaning woman came on Wednesday.) He watched as
Sophie and Benjamin whispered their goodbyes, foreheads pressed
together as if they were holding one another up.

When Benjamin finally left, Walter was cross with her. For her
beauty, for everything that sparkled in and about her, for what she did
not see and could not help. He hated himself for it, but he had to ask.

"Sophie, who are all these people? And why are they all so," he
searched for his meaning, "beholden to you?"

"Oh, just some friends of mine," she said. "I have lots and lots of
friends, Walter. Good news! It's time for you to select your Internet
identity. This is my favorite part."

"I like my given name," Walter said. He was pouting, and didn't
care that she saw.

"As do I, but it's already spoken for in the virtual world, Walter. Most names are. You are too late now, I'm afraid, to be Walter
Bombardier." Sophie's amusement with this fact agitated Walter.

Not cross with her, now, but despairing. Because this girl
already had such a surplus of love directed her way, she would never
need a thing from a man like him.

"I don't know," he said, "anything will do, I suppose."

"That's not the spirit at all. You've come this far, Walter, now
stay the course, will you? I can help you choose something, if you
like." Walter did want to know, what would Sophie decide suited
him? "Let's free associate or something. Just throw out some words.
I know! What do you like most in the world? What makes you the best
Walter Bombardier of all the Walter Bombardiers?"

Walter could think of nothing that he was willing to say out loud,
"This is nonsense."

"Books, Walter! Right? Come on, now," she wasn't mocking
him, she was trying to be kind, "books are your one true love."

"Yes, that's right," he said, grateful.

"So, you just relax. This is why you hired me! I'll just play
around with that concept for a while," Sophie said, turning back.

Walter liked watching her shoulders as she sat working at his keyboard. Nothing about her was not lovely. He asked her increasingly complex questions (she was very bright; she was beyond him now) just to keep her talking.

After a while, Sophie said, "Well, mark my words: they'll be using DNA someday, you know. Instead of silicone. In the chips."

Walter was so enjoying the cadence of Sophie's voice, feeling her pitch vibrate in the shafts of hair at the base of his skull. Until now, the content had been only perplexing ramblings to him.

"Did you say DNA? But that's perverse," he said, "Maybe you heard that wrong. They must have meant DNA replications. Synthetic DNA, or something."

"No, Walter. DNA is DNA! And you might as well know this about me right now: I say what I mean. I think using DNA is a brilliant idea. Much better than nanotechnology. The stuff is abundant, obviously, not to mention pristine. And it's quite inexpensive, you should appreciate that."

Walter told Sophie that, no, he did not. He told her that machines were created to do the work of man. He wasn't sure how or when he had come to this, but he was afraid. Because it seemed to him what ought to remain based upon convenience, and, well perhaps discovery and invention to some degree as well, he supposed, was evolving (unchecked) toward something dangerously close to reliance, necessity, and even submission.

"So now you tell me that one day living things, no, worse than that, the *essence* of living things will be used to do the work of machines? It's nothing to be glib about, Sophie. It's very disturbing."

Sophie was looking at Walter, and her face seemed to take something in.

"It is quite, isn't it Walter? Thank you for that new thought you have given me." He believed that she meant this. "Now, back to my work," she said, and turned back to the screen.

Walter sat resting in his favorite chair with a puzzle book on this lap while he waited for Sophie to name him. The afternoon sun was warm. He must have dozed off, because Sophie's voice woke him like a harsh alarm.

"No, No, No! This isn't working!"

"Do you need something?" he asked her, longing to fetch another strange treat that she might relish.

"No. This is serious, Walter. We need to talk about your intentions," she said. His desire was showing. She suspected him, and rightly so.

"My intentions?" he asked.

"Yes. Why are you getting connected? Why now?" Sophie did not mean his longing. (Wasn't she, after all, what he longed for?) But if Sophie had meant his ambition, this he could explain.

"I plan to trade in books on the Internet, remember? It seems to be the way that things are done today, and I don't want to miss out."

"That's really what you are after with all of this?"

Walter felt convicted. Did she know that he never resold the books that he had purchased ostensibly for that purpose? That he never actually read them, either? But now, who did this coffee shop girl think that she was? He had hired her. His dealings were not relevant to their arrangement. Sophie was making everything too complicated, and confusing him with her persistent (intrusive!) questions.

"Yes, of course!" he said, "I already explained this to you."

"Because I'm not feeling it, Walter," she said, "My third eye is all itchy, and it's refusing to open up for you. No offense."

Walter nodded. None taken.

She went on, "And also, this is very strange, I'm not getting any sort of sign on a name for you, either. Nothing. This *never* happens to me, Walter."

She looked plain and small now that something was troubling her. Sophie was packing up her things. This sort of drama was appealing only to the young. They were here, in Walter's apartment. She was trying to invent something more. They were not waiting for a portent or some spiritual transfiguration, like Sophie was fussing about. The girl had a job to do and her charming eccentricities were becoming less so.

She told him, "You know what? To tell you the truth, I haven't slept for a few days. Maybe my energy is all messed up. Maybe if I sleep for a few hours. I'll call you."

"Well," he said. (The girl hadn't slept in a few days? She needed a good night's sleep, for heaven's sake.) "I'll just keep thinking about that name while you're gone, then." He was waiting, hoping that, after all this, Sophie would offer an affectionate ritual to bid him farewell.

"I'm out of here," she said, giving him only an ineffectual peace sign as she closed the door.

That night, Walter missed her company. The apartment missed her, the chair. He tried to imagine Sophie back at her work. It was only the notion of her, there at his dining room table, which allowed him to finally fall asleep. When Walter's phone woke him, his mind worked quickly through his short list of acquaintances that might have died in the night.

"You lied to me."

It was Sophie.

"What? Sophie?"

"You told me a lie, Walter. About your intentions."

It was two in the morning.

"I don't understand," he said, "I didn't lie about anything." Nothing important. Nothing of any consequence.

"Oh yes you did, Walter, and I am very mad at you," she was ablaze now with something unrecognizable. "What we have here is either your basic act of vengeance or a quest for a rare-slash-precious object or a rightful re-acquisition situation. Maybe even all three. I'm still not clear. Because I have to sort through all of your bullshit, Walter! Do you have any idea how infuriating that is?"

Walter acknowledged that, indeed, he did not. He had no idea what she was talking about. She was frenetic.

"Anyway, that doesn't even matter. The point is that I have totally different fee structures for those sorts of things." She was not in her right mind. Walter needed to talk her down.

"Sophie, listen. I'm sorry, really I am. Where are you? Are you alright?"

"Oh, no you don't! Do not patronize me, Walter. I can *so* keep pace with you. Understand?"

Walter did know that. She outran him in thought, and deed. "Yes, yes. I understand," he said, to calm her, to bring her back toward him, to give himself a few seconds to make some sense of this.

"Very good. Now, I've spoken with Delaney. I know that sneaky buyer's name and home address."

"Wait. Delaney? How do you know him? Sophie, what is going on here?" Whatever this was, she was scaring him. Whatever this was, it was quickly becoming out of his control.

"Oh, Walter, Walter. You are such a dear. There are elaborate networks of righteousness at work. You simply have no idea." He had to get away, right now, before someone got hurt.

"Listen, I think we had better call off our arrangement, Sophie. I will pay you fairly, of course, for all your time and effort. How does four hundred sound?" She was quiet. Walter wanted to believe that they were almost through.

"Walter!" Sophie sounded for a moment like the pretty girl who had sat at his dining room table that afternoon, "I just figured you out!" Had she? What did that even mean? "You had absolutely no idea what you really wanted, did you? Poor you, Walter. That's very sad, but it explains everything."

What he wanted, now, was to be done with her. For her to hang up the phone. For both of them to get some sleep.

"Listen," Walter told her, "why don't I stop in for coffee tomorrow? In fact, I'll bring your check. Did we agree on four hundred?" He could almost feel the grip on his throat, his heart, release.

"Now, Walter. You're a smart man. I think we've established that, don't you? Your lack of self-awareness just means that I can forgive you. Just don't tell me any more lies! I still have my job to do."

"I'll see you back here tomorrow, then? For my official naming ceremony and navigation lesson?" Walter could not imagine what she had in mind, and was afraid to try.

"You must know better than that. I'll see you when I'm all through."

"Please!" Walter said as she hung up, "Get some sleep!"

Walter woke early and went to Mick's with a check already made out to "Sophie" for four hundred dollars. He did not know Sophie's last name, and would need to add it when her saw her. He brought along his checkbook as well, just in case she demanded more. And he would gladly pay it.

But she was not working when he arrived, and so he asked the regular girl when Sophie's next shift would be.

"We don't have a Sophie here," she said.

Walter did not doubt that Sophie had gotten herself fired. (She was unpredictable, volatile.) But he owed the girl money. She had made it very clear last night how unwise it would be to betray her.

"She'll be back at some point, I'm sure, to pick up her last paycheck? I just have something I need to leave here for her."

"No one named Sophie works here. Or worked here. Get it?" the regular girl told him. Walter still didn't understand, "As in, we've never had a Sophie working here. Ev-er, OK?"

Walter remembered Sophie's disguise, a private deception that she had shared just with him. Why, even the regular girl wasn't privy to it!

"Of course, of course. Silly me. I'm looking for Jennie."

The regular girl frowned, and pointed above her small left breast where her nametag was pinned.

"I'm Jennie," she said. It was the same pin that Sophie had worn at her throat.

"Come on now, this isn't funny. Sophie was working here just the day before yesterday, in the morning, when you're usually here. She was even wearing your nametag, as a gag. She's been at my apartment and I owe her four hundred dollars for services rendered."

The real Jennie crossed her arms across her chest, "Listen, mister, I don't know anything about any of that. Do you want to order something or not?"

"Fine," Walter said. He still had the punch card with Sophie's cell phone number written on it. He would get some coffee and go home and hope that the best version of Sophie would answer the line when he called.

"I'll just have the usual," Walter began digging out the exact coins for his small cup of dark roast. But the real Jennie just looked at him, and let out a long sigh.

"OK, Mister. And what would that be?"

Now she was acting as if she didn't recognize Walter or know his usual order. She had to, of course, because Walter came in every morning. And there were even times when he and real Jennie, now that he thought about it, had occasionally shared what might be called a teasing banter. She was just playing with him!

"Think way, way back," Walter said, "to the day before the day before yesterday." He winked, just to be clear.

"Do I need to call a manager up here?" This could not be right. How could she not know him?

"But, I come in every day. I've seen you at least two hundred times, I'll bet." Walter felt as if he were sinking.

"I'm really sorry," she said. She looked at Walter now, like she might actually be. Sorry. For him. And he didn't want that. He didn't want any of it.

"Never mind," Walter said, "one small dark roast. To go, please." He handed the real Jennie his coins.

Halfway home Walter heard the spiral cry of sirens. On any other day, the sound would have nothing to do with him, but this was unlike any other day. His body knew, and he began to run, his thin legs straining to remember how, stopping where Delaney's store was supposed to be. Instead, Walter's eyes were captivated by the ravishing blaze, the smoke rising up in the most unassuming shade of blue.

Walter found his apartment door opened and Sophie waiting for him on his sofa. He was not surprised. She had a small coil of cable on her lap.

"Why hello, Walter."

Walter grabbed her slim shoulders, forcing her to stand up and face him.

"I think I like it when you're rough."

"Stop that," he said, to Sophie, to himself, "What on earth have you done?"

"Easy enough. You're offline now, Walter," she held up an end of the cable.

"I mean Delaney's. I mean *Delaney!*" Walter told her. She laughed. How could she still sound good to him?

"You're hurting my feelings, now, Walter. I'm not a murderer. No one gets hurt. I couldn't abide such a thing. It was just a fire. OK, fine. There was some significant property damage. Someone might suspect arson. Maybe insurance won't pay out. But that's all."

She was raising her hand toward his face, placing the back of it against his brow.

"What are you doing, Sophie?" he said. How could he welcome her touch, even now?

"Your face is hot. It's kind of nice," Sophie said.

She was standing so close to him now. Walter hated himself for wanting her.

"Now, I have a surprise for you. But you must close your eyes and hold out your hands."

Walter did exactly as he was told. He felt Sophie take his wrists, space his hands apart, just so, and face his palms toward one another.

"Ready?" she asked him.

If it were possible to hold something in spirit, to sense the shape and weight of an object before the truth of it rested in your hands, Walter knew. An inch away and seconds before. He opened his eyes to see Sophie standing expectantly before him and looked down at what she had given him.

"It's my *Le Morte d'Arthur*," Walter opened the book with care, turned it over gently. It was so beautiful.

"Finally, Walter!" Sophie was jubilant now, "I can see you! In all your splendid chivalry."

To feel what he did for this girl, it was reckless beyond measure. If Walter had believed in God, this moment might have been his most fervent prayer.

"Sophie, how did you get this book?"

"The old-fashioned way, of course," she said, and she winked.

Suddenly Walter's hands, his body, felt beyond empty. He had to sit down.

"You know something? I really like you, Walter. I have no idea why. I like you even more than that sneaky buyer, and you should have seen how nice I had to be to him."

Walter felt the weight of a new and unbearable sorrow.

"Please, say something, won't you?"

Walter sat, the book resting on his lap, his face in his hands.

"Are you overcome? Sometimes people are overcome, and I really like that for some reason," she said, and when he said nothing, "I'll take that as a Yes. And you are most welcome."

She kissed the top of his head and began to gather her things. Walter did not want her to leave. He wanted Sophie to keep talking, keep touching, longer than any services could possibly be rendered. He wanted her to stay with him, in his apartment, with her voice and all her peculiar and frightening beauty. Walter lifted his face.

"Wait," he said. She was already at the door.

"For you, Sire, gratis," she said, and gave him a courtly bow.

"Please, stay," he said.

"Walter," she said, "my work here is done."

"No, I want you to stay. And read it to me."

"You want me to stay?" she asked.

"Oh, Walter," she said.

"Please," Walter said. Yes, he would gladly be the fool for her. But she did not laugh.

"Please," he said, again, "start at the beginning."

Sophie went into his kitchen and helped herself to a tall glass of grapefruit juice. She turned off her cell phone, drew the blinds against the day, and sat down next to him.

"Walter, do you have any idea how much this is going to cost you?"

He did, he understood completely.

She told him, come on then. Rest your head here, in my lap. Which he did, like a boy, yielding.

PSYCHIC SUZY TELLS ME THE FUTURE

When I was a boy of twelve, in my ardent desire to avoid blaspheming the Holy Spirit, I sought the council of my classmate and unchurched neighbor girl, Psychic Suzy. I had recently returned from my summer Bible camp where I had *not* been filled with the spirit, had *not* spoken in tongues—though I believed that I had faked it convincingly enough for my young brothers and sisters—and most troubling: I had *not* felt the call to either ministry or missionary work on my young life. I had, however, found the food most wholesome and satisfying.

Back at home Suzy had been practicing the art of palmistry since school let out in June, and by mid-August was prepared (for a nominal fee) to divine the future of any child-customer from a station on her back porch. I knew this because Suzy's grubby twin brothers had been distributing advertisements all week, but only when they finally (reluctantly) delivered the last one to me as they pedaled past my driveway into their own could I believe that I, too, was welcome.

I needed a sign and this was it.

My Baptist mother had succinctly declared Suzy "trouble" years ago, so I would be on morally dangerous ground just talking to the girl. Consulting Suzy in matters of the occult was far worse. I knew better. But I was desperate, you see. Thanks to a legalistic youth pastor and my own neurotic predilections, I had firmly attached myself to a new obsession with the notion of The Unforgivable Sin, that is

"Blaspheming the Holy Spirit." The misguided youth pastor strikes me now as a young man full of sorrow and fear and inaccurate teaching. At my current post, I'd send the poor soul to a good therapist straight away and wouldn't think of hiring him on in a leadership role. But at the time, before I'd found my faith and with no one to tell me otherwise, his words held such sway over me that I was convinced I was bound for Hell if I somehow *missed* the Holy Spirit's call, if I somehow managed to *ignore* the Holy Spirit. And I was under such duress: what if I was busy reading a comic, or sleeping, or (please no, not this, however likely it might have been) pleasuring myself, and I simply didn't *catch* what the Holy Spirit was trying to tell me?

I was too young to imagine that any of my faithful campmates suffered such doubt, as I had, and I felt utterly alone. Suzy had provided an invitation to participate (knowingly) in what my mother would most certainly call sin. But it was a *forgivable* sin—covered with the blood—and it would enable me, I reasoned, to avoid unintentionally committing The Unforgivable Sin: blowing off the marching orders of the Holy Spirit and choosing the *wrong* profession.

Palm Reading by Psychic Suzy

$1 per session

No discounts!

Yell into house through the back door <u>before dinner</u> for appointment.

Satisfaction Guaranteed!

I did not know when a family like Suzy's ate dinner. Ours ate promptly at five-thirty every evening, so I showed up at five hoping it would be acceptable. The back porch was dark and the torn screen on the door was rolled up against the frame, secured with assorted patches of duct tape. I called in to Suzy as instructed.

"Hello?" Nothing. I tried again.

"Hello? Suzy?" Again, nothing.

I looked down at my hands, considering my eternal damnation. When I looked up again Suzy was standing just inside the door looking out at me. I was ready for magic and so was certain that she had simply appeared.

"Hey," Suzy wiped her hands on her cut-off jean shorts. "I was in the john taking a crap."

Undeterred, I offered her one dollar of my lawn mowing money through the open frame. She didn't take it.

"Does your crazy mother know you're here?"

I didn't like hearing her assessment aloud, although I had overheard it often enough. Even then, I was beginning to suspect the truth of it myself.

"No, she doesn't."

"Good." Suzy reached out and took my dollar, which she promptly shoved into a margarine container and placed under her chair. "Well, you should know: you're lucky."

I smiled at her, because I *felt* lucky. And hopeful, and possibility, and promise that I understood—just then—had been dulled in me for some time.

"I'm closing up shop after you."

I offered Suzy my upturned hand and held my breath as she examined my palm.

"That's surprising."

"What?"

"You have artistic tendencies."

"What does that mean?"

"Oh, wait."

"What?"

"Pity."

"What's a pity? Me?"

"You lack courage. That's so sad. Why do you lack courage?"

"I don't know."

"Listen, kid," (Suzy was six months my junior) "this could go either way, but good luck!"

"That's it? That's a rip off! You didn't tell me my future. You didn't tell me *anything!*"

"Well, you're kinda cute," she was clearly sizing me up. "For another buck, I'll show you my titties?"

"No thanks!" Suzy looked offended, which was not my intent. I appreciated the offer, but was there on serious business. "Thanks, anyway. I just need to know what I should be when I grow up. I need to know my *calling!*"

"Jeez! Don't be pissed at me because you have weak lines! I didn't *build* you."

"Suzy, please?"

"I *guess* I could try again." Suzy turned her face away from me but held out her margarine container.

"Fine." I deposited my last dollar, and Suzy held my hand again.

She took her time, tracing the lines on my palm with her index finger.

"Do you really want to know?" Her tone had such foreboding, her eyes such genuine concern, for a moment I wasn't sure. But I had come this far.

"Yes. I *have* to know."

She nodded.

"I'm afraid that you will be a grave disappointment to your crazy mother. A *grave* disappointment."

I dropped my head. What form would this take? I admit that I took some horrible satisfaction imagining a nasty assortment of ways that I could, apparently would, disappoint my mother.

"*Buh-uht!*" Suzy chimed. (Please understand; there is no other fitting word!)

I saw what a pretty girl Suzy was when she smiled. One day, though I couldn't know it then, she would be quite beautiful. There would be a time, late in high school and my first summer home from Wheaton College, that I would be simply mad for Suzy. But as is common, I met and married another, a kind woman who still makes me laugh and keeps me sane. And all these years later, I am almost certain that Suzy never loved me in return.

There on that hot summer day, just outside her back screen door, I was waiting for Suzy to proclaim my future. She was positively beaming at me and, more than anything, I was ready to believe her prophecy:

"You. Will. Be. Happy."

WHAT THE UNIVERSE TELLS MARTA

Marta always felt gloriously pissed off after her Tuesday/Thursday morning yoga class. She knew this was not the point of yoga class. It was good to inhabit the body, and Marta was supposed to be practicing the art of attentiveness. During her final arch up from the hardwood floor, she couldn't help but notice that her arms were certainly longer, one might even use the word lithe. She felt a lovely, tiny pond of sweat center itself in the curve of her back, rest there, cooling at the base of her spine.

A woman on Marta's right let out a deliberate sigh. She was wrapped in fabric of mustard and sage, "What is the most difficult form of yoga, do you know?"

There were degrees of yoga? Marta hadn't realized, "Not really."

"It's just that," the woman said, "well, this is a little low key, don't you think?"

Marta placed a small towel around her neck. The woman was asking her something. She ought to respond.

"I think it's fine," Marta slipped on her shoes and took a long drink of water, a form of goodbye. But the woman waited for her and walked Marta out to the eighth-floor landing.

"I always take the stairs," the woman said.

So did Marta. Everyone did, for the cardio and their glutes. But today Marta saw an old elevator and wondered why she had never noticed it before. The gilded door seemed eager and relevant, like an artifact just now discovered. Marta pressed the word "DOWN", turned to the woman and lied, "I must have strained something."

"Well, I won't be here Thursday," the woman called out. And then, in a stage whisper, "Too easy for me!"

"Goodbye then," Marta said as she stepped aboard, "and good luck." Inside, Marta pushed the number "1" and leaned against the thick brass rail behind her. The woman waved, Marta waved back, the solid doors closed.

The elevator car had been beautiful once. Worn scarlet brocade dressed the four walls and Marta touched one of the large covered buttons. Looking up she saw half of her face in the mirrored ceiling, spliced by the cut and design. But there she was (part of her anyway) framed by a circle of yellow lights. She didn't look bad. The motor above the elevator car engaged.

Marta was sure to have just enough time for a shower and coffee before beginning work, and this fact pleased her. She no longer found her routine confining. Regarding work, Marta had resolved that an average person should not expect pleasure or integrity in an average day.

Marta liked to remember getting high with her favorite lab partner for a few months during graduate school. They usually had sex afterward. She had loved him for a time, and he had tried his best to know her.

Him: What would you do if you could do anything at all?

Her: You mean, for my job?

Him: That's not what I asked, Marta, but go ahead, for your job.

Her: What did you ask? Can you repeat the question?

Him: It's not an oral exam, Marta. What would you do, if you could do anything?

Her: I've never thought about it. I don't know. What about you?

Him: I would hold my breath and excavate Atlantis.

Her: Something like that? You mean imaginary things?

Him: Jeez, Marta. You're making me so sad.

He had gone to Memphis to lead research at St. Jude's in cord-blood stem cell use for the treatment of childhood leukemia. Marta had stayed in St. Paul to work as a chemist at 3M for the advancement and improvement of adhesive materials. Marta wished that she, too, possessed the fortitude for such unabashed goodness. She had tried volunteering as a Guardian Ad Litem in family court. It was her job to think of the children but she found that she could not sleep at night, thinking of them. She had to quit before she grew irrevocably ashamed of her many comforts.

Sometimes it was useful to pretend that her job was only temporary. Other times it was necessary to engage the imagination. An element was nothing if not an ancient thing, hidden but permanent. Wasn't it old Empedocles who said it? Every object (yoga mat, Scotch Tape, Marta) was made up of just four elements: earth, air, fire, water. Marta's own work as a chemist, then, was rather like a form of elemental archeology. Most great discoveries were not made by endeavor, but by accident. Even Dr. Harry Coover had discovered "Superglue" by mistake. (It had only taken the man sixteen years to realize what he had.) A person really just had to keep on. And pay attention. This very elevator, here, was going about its work. Unchangeable physics, the principle of weight and counterweights were the only things holding her up, and the very things promising to bring Marta safely to the ground. This elevator ride might serve as an affirmation of Marta's circumstance: Her home in St. Paul, yoga on days beginning with a "t," her work for the last fourteen years.

On six the elevator stopped so that a man and woman could board. Marta chided herself for assuming that she might enjoy a solitary ride, and cursed the frequency of her self-induced disappointments. The man and woman were each dressed for their particular form of work. The woman wore a pale blue skirt and matching jacket, along with real panty hose. An administrative assistant.

The man's coveralls could make him a custodian or possibly an electrician.

"Oh, hello there," the assistant said.

Marta backed up and nodded a greeting.

"Good morning," the man said to both of them.

The assistant replied by pressing the "1" button (it was already lit) with five insistent pokes. "Come on, come on," she said to the door. "Cigarette break," she told Marta, (as if in confidence) "only fifteen minutes." The assistant looked the man up and down, "Dare I ask what you're doing here?"

The man smiled. Marta noticed the rectangular patch above his left shirt pocket. It read: "Plunkett's." She had been wrong.

"Exterminator?" Marta asked.

"That's right, ladies," the man said, "And you don't want to know."

"Oh, but we do," the assistant said.

Marta did not want any more details, actually. She did not want to remember the multitude of brown earwigs that had shared her first basement apartment in St. Paul. But of course that wish recalled them clearly. They wore a set of pinchers where their faces ought to have been. Legend was, the earwig had earned its name by crawling into the unsuspecting ears of sleeping humans, burrowing and digging, eventually taking up residence in the brain. Over time, they drove their host mad. A myth, debunked, naturally. But unwelcome thoughts could infest the mind, so Marta chose to sleep with her earplugs in place until she moved out.

"Okay then," the man, the exterminator, said, "Just how much rain did we get this spring, do you suppose?"

"Rain, rain. We know. Plenty of it," said the assistant.

Marta knew that water was certainly not the official element of spring. That was air. She had gone camping with a lover one spring, and they had encountered an unrelenting rain. When he had tried to pitch their tent, the stakes would not take hold in the earth. What do you think, Marta? (That's what he had said.) I saw some nice little cabins up there near the front gate. Marta had liked his neck and the smell of his hair, but she did not admire him. (Now Marta wondered why she had so quickly acquiesced. Why had she slept with him that night, and stayed with him another three months?) Nothing wrong with a couple of rookies like us moving to higher ground.

"This past spring," the exterminator told them, "is one for the record books. Let's just put it that way. Nowhere else for them to go but up, if you know what I mean."

"What?" the assistant asked, "Who?"

Marta watched the numbers above the door lighting up as the car began to carry them down. Why were they all still suspended here? Marta heard a steel cable, wrapped tight around its sheave. Then a pulley began to turn. During yoga class, she was supposed to imagine her mind where it usually lived, right behind her eyes. This she could do. But the rest was difficult work.

The assistant told him, "Quit stalling, and tell us what you are after here."

"Okay then, but don't say I didn't warn you. So, we've got several reports of rats coming up through the toilets. They figure the sewers must be flooding."

"You have got to be kidding," the assistant said.

"Afraid not," he seemed to be enjoying this.

"You mean to say," said the assistant, "that I might just sit down, only to get bitten on the backside by a rat?"

He laughed. "Well, well. I never thought of that! But you really shouldn't worry. We're pretty sure they've only gotten as far as the fourth floor. Although, I wouldn't blame the little fellow, if he wanted to meet you. After seeing your backside." He winked, and the assistant smiled. For that she gave him a playful, gentle slap on the forearm (naughty boy!) but she let her hand rest there, just for a second.

Marta had never gotten very far during the last part of yoga practice, trying to move her mind down to her heart. It was hard enough, just to remain in the body. The body contained four humors: black bile, blood, yellow bile, phlegm. The humors matched the elements: earth, air, fire, water. The elements were ancient. And what was the body? What was her body, a temple, a ruin?

"So, what will you do with them, once you find them?" the assistant asked.

"The rats? Oh, we know how to rout them out. Listen, I don't know how high they'll climb, but you're really probably fine up there near the top."

When would they finally reach the ground? She tried to imagine being a rat, traversing the brackish waterways under the city, the rising tide, finding her way in the dark to the network of pipes beneath them now. Who could have predicted such a distance? Marta could return, on her own, to that final exercise. She had to be getting close.

The assistant had a soft pack of "Camel Lights" in her hand, ready to go. She asked the exterminator, "Smoke?"

"No thanks, but I'd love to join you when we get outside," he said.

The next step for Marta was to close her eyes, turn her mind into an elevator car, and push it all the way to the back of her head.

In the end, the body could not be avoided.

(Mind. Eyes. Car. Yes.)

Marta knew that much.

(Elevator. Mind. Car. Yes.)

Her spine. Her spine could be a functioning elevator shaft.

(Spine? Spine. Shaft. Yes.)

She could move her mind down, she could.

(Down. Down. Down. Down.)

She could move her mind down, through every element, down.

(Now, move, mind, move!)

And there she was. (There she was!) Closing in on her heart.

When Marta opened her eyes, she felt the elevator car set down. The doors opened, and the exterminator gestured grandly with his arm.

"After you," he said. Marta saw the assistant step across the threshold like a maiden. The exterminator reached out to her and the two of them moved forward, arm in arm, as the spring air pressed against the heat of their luminous skin.

DON'T TELL ME HOW THIS STORY ENDS

The week before David turned seventy years old, Frances decided she would become a good daughter. Her father was aging. Left knee replaced, a minor stroke. That was his job now, to age. And as his daughter, Frances was to rise above any unresolved resentments. Luckily, David was becoming forgetful and weak, and this seemed to be prompting her toward forgiveness.

Frances called her father on the evening of his birthday, after a long run and a glass of pinot noir.

"David," she said, "Happy Birthday." That was it.

"Frannie, you remembered!" Though she had outgrown it long ago, and always hated it, her father still called her Frannie.

"Well, of course." Could she really already be working this hard?

"If I was an old horse," he said, she'd heard this one, "they'd have shot me by now." Frances laughed. She couldn't help it. Her father had always been funny, if caustic.

"Well, I've got a present for you that I'll bet you didn't even know you wanted. How about a trip up to the North Shore next weekend? I already have a nice site at Split Rock reserved. What do you think?"

"Like when you were kids. Are the boys coming?"

She thought he must be joking again. Adam and Alex were forever "the boys" to David. From the beginning of time, it seemed all their names were to be spoken in a particular order: Adam, Alex,

Frannie. Was it by age, or rank? (How Frances had wanted to be good enough for her father. Years of therapy and dysfunctional relationships to learn this: her father would not change.) She was never really in the running anyway, given her innocuous genitalia and position in their birth order. No one could expect, nor could she aspire, to be anything but a girl coming in last place. Adam and Alex had come first, identical twins with the proper appendages, and even from the initial ride of their lives fought to be the first one down and out. Neither baby had stepped aside, resulting in a long morphine-induced nap and an emergency C-section for their terminally sad mother. When the boys became men they had swiftly left St. Paul for opposite coasts, leaving behind an unspoken rivalry born of David's conditional affections.

They had not always come to Split Rock. Once there was an Uncle Mike and a standing invitation for their family to his lake home every summer. Toward evening one of those summer days, all of their bodies waterlogged and thankful that the day was finally coming to an end, David had asked, "You don't have another ski rope?" And Uncle Mike began setting the boys up behind the boat to water-ski together. He offered to drive so that David and Frances could really watch the show, the Grand Finale, he'd said. David sat in front and Frances faced back, the spotter, to alert Uncle Mike if the boys wanted anything (faster, slower, just right) or if one of them went down. The boat circled the small lake once and Uncle Mike closed in on the shore, ready to bring Adam and Alex around near the dock at a gentle speed for a graceful landing. David climbed into the back with Frances. He was a large man and the weight of him shifted the boat. He took the other rear-facing seat and motioned to the boys: a wide circle with his index finger raised—didn't they want to go around just one more time? Adam and Alex shook their heads in unison, no. Frances saw it.

But David had called up to Uncle Mike, "Wait, they say don't go in just yet." Uncle Mike laughed, pulled away from the curve of shore and resumed his speed. The boys were animals! They circled the lake twice more. It was time for the adults to start their overdue cocktail hour. Frances heard the deep ring of the old fire bell sounding, serving as the call for dinner. She said softly, "Dinner."

"Yes," Uncle Mike said, but was looking to David, "You know, Buddy, those boys have to be pretty spent. They've been at it all day."

"We'll just see how long they last," David said, and when Frances turned to him, surprised, he set his jaw. Frances knew what this was. A challenge to her loyalty and a test for her brothers.

The boys knew it, too. Adam and Alex held on to their ropes, joyless and steadfast, as dusk descended. Frances had wanted to say something innocent and magical. She understood that this was possible, that this was part of her power as a young and pretty girl, to bring both the men back to their senses with words like: "I'm really hungry," or "It's getting dark."

But this time, she didn't dare. She was also well acquainted with the unpredictable nature of times like these, and could recognize when the adults who were supposed to be in charge were preparing to make strange and dangerous choices which she was powerless to stop.

Neither Adam nor Alex lost, but nobody won. When the boat finally ran out of gas, Uncle Mike began to pull Adam in toward the boat with his ski rope. He motioned Frances to do the same for Alex. Frances had obeyed her uncle, until her father stood over her, placing his hand on the rope.

"The boys can swim, you know," he told Uncle Mike, which only made Uncle Mike pull Adam in even faster.

Frances knew which man was right, but the other man was her father, so she had dropped her rope and watched Alex swim in.

"Tie," David announced, though no one but him was satisfied.

Uncle Mike and Adam paddled the boat to the dock in silence, and their family was not invited back again.

It made Frances sad to imagine her brothers now, each standing precariously on his edge, as far from each other as possible without falling into his respective ocean.

Of course, she took her father's question as a poor attempt at dark humor—laughed for his sake—at the notion that the boys might be joining them on the same weekend, might be joining them at all. When David didn't laugh with her, Frances tried a partial truth.

"It's just been so long. I didn't even think to invite them."

After their first night together at Split Rock, Frances woke early. The inner wall of orange nylon next to her was wet and cold. The sun was still quite low, and she needed some kind of ritual to ground her. She wanted to take a run, to make coffee, to watch the waves hit the rocks for a while. She was old enough to know what she needed now. An hour to herself before she had to be nice to anyone, particularly to David. Frances read from her squat daily meditation books, *Living with Grace* and *Words of Wisdom for Women*. She hated the fact that she needed such basic reassurance to sustain her, affirmations like: "I choose to be empowered today," and "I can be good to myself." It was embarrassing.

When she emerged from the zipper-door of her tent, David startled her, standing by the circle of stones where they would later build their fire.

"You're up early," she said.

"I was thinking about pancakes."

"Right," she said, a memory dawning. Her mother had made them. "We always ate pancakes."

Here she was, in the middle of one of the few family traditions that she could name. When Frances was a girl, they had camped at Split Rock State Park nearly every summer for many years. There were no plans, no family activities, but they were all together. Things were quiet, and even. Frances remembered the way she and her brothers had taken off their shoes. She loved the solid cold beneath her feet. The children would climb the huge black rocks along the water for hours. (Even as a girl, Frances saw now, she had to be forced to find a literal balance.) They had moved with a common purpose then, like they were working toward something pressing and real. In those days, their silence had been simple and mutual. It was the closest she had ever come to reverence. Maybe this was why she had to bring David.

His fancy for pancakes became her duty, and Frances set about her tasks with determined generosity. All told, it took her forty-five minutes just to get started: set up the camp stove, heat the skillet, mix some "Jiffy" and water with a small plastic fork, break several tines, and pick shards of white plastic from the batter. David was watching her now, just standing around, and she wanted a way to connect with him.

"David," she said, "I need the spatula. Can you dig in that box for the spatula?"

He looked pleased to have a job, to be needed. His head disappeared as he rummaged through the box. From inside he pronounced, "Don't you worry, sweetheart. If there is any worrying to be done in this family, I'll take care of it."

Those words were lovely, but they didn't belong to her father. Frances thought she recognized the cadence. Maybe it had been Atticus Finch comforting his beloved Scout in her favorite book, *To Kill a Mockingbird*. Or, stepfather Mike Brady from an episode of the seventies' sitcom "The Brady Bunch," upon entering the sanctity of the girls' pubescent pink room to speak with them about their troubles. Frances had wished for a man like that to be her father. When David had been home, he said things like, "Buck up!" and "What's that? Did you say something, Frannie?" and first thing in the morning, "Holy shit, my head might as well split in two."

"Got it!" David said. He was triumphantly holding up the spatula, and Frances thanked him.

Frances created a stack of eleven nice pancakes and threw several burned ones to a group of raucous gulls. (She only liked them from a distance.) She covered the pancakes with foil, resigning herself to apricot jam after realizing that she had forgotten the syrup. When she was finished and the coffee was hot, Frances looked forward to making David happy. They were going to share a meal together. That morning, Frances had felt a crooked kind of hope in her gut. It was so old and familiar—she almost mistook it for hunger. Now it was time to eat, but she could not find David. Frances checked around their camp, and waited. She walked down to the shore. She waited. Frances was proud of the fact that she knew how to wait. She watched the dirty white gulls press against the blue, the waves and clouds moving in frantic ways, etching their power into the water and sky. After another half hour, she broke a private vow she had made not to use her cell phone that weekend and called the Split Rock Lighthouse Museum.

"I am looking for my father," she said. A gift shop girl with a thin voice took down her number in case David wandered in. He had been gone another full hour when Frances started to feel unwell. It was the sort of unease born of tragedy or guilt. Like the back wheel of her car had just hit a large stray dog. Like she had just told her lover a terrible lie.

Then David walked into their campsite, beaming. His hair was wet.

"Where were you?" Frances asked. "I was seriously worried." He was alive and fine. This was the luxury, available only to her now that he was safe, permitting her fear to transcend into fury. "I made your pancakes, David. Two hours ago."

Frances could not help herself, her arm reaching out, forcing David to see the pretty stack of pancakes. She felt both right and ridiculous, like a pitiful wife with a late, ungrateful husband and a perfectly good roast, ruined.

"Frannie!" David was missing all the wrath she was directing his way. He was simply delighted to see her. "What a girl! I just had the most glorious walk. Glorious! Oh, soup's on."

Frances could practice forgiveness, here and now. It was called a process. Part of a process could be a long walk in the middle of a forgotten breakfast. David sat down and began to eat his pancakes. They had to be cold. He started to drink his coffee. Frances took his cup and warmed it up for him. She was gathering herself. A walk was a walk. A walk was not her father's habitual stormy nights in her youth, her dead mother, the metallic smell of scotch. These things were obvious. A walk was not a house full of hate.

David was busy describing the rhythm of the waves, as though they were something brand new to them both. He showed Frances the agate in his pocket, ate with fervor.

"Look at this Frannie!" he said. "Really look, will you? I found us a winner." He showed her the same agate, again. Then, enthusiastically between large mouthfuls, redundant compliments. "Frannie, these pancakes are terrific, terrific! Apricot jam!"

"David!" she stopped him. He was really being foolish. "Please do not do that to me again."

He looked at her. His pale eyes right into her own, and Frances did not like it one bit.

"Frannie, have I ever told you how much you look like your mother?" Her mother had left him after twenty years of marriage. Before and since, David had many other women.

"That's not funny, David."

"Well, she is quite a beauty, you know," he said. Her father was taking this too far.

"You know mom's been gone for ten years, David. What are you talking about?" At this bad news, Frances saw a cloud cross over her father's face, but just for a moment, and then he was grinning at her once again.

Peculiar incidents, scattered between them the past several months, came into alarming focus for her now. She should have paid better attention: David's cat left out for two days. His toilet overflowing. A few nonsensical phone calls, late at night, which

Frances just remembered, this moment, like an ongoing series of uncharted dreams. She did not know what this was. Another stroke? Some kind of residual dementia? Something was seriously wrong with her father.

Frances considered what a good daughter might do. First, she would recognize a serious situation and take action. She would know what medications her father was currently taking. Maybe even his doctor's name. She would not panic at the thought of going into her father's apartment, looking for an address book, a stack of bills, or a skinny cat. A good daughter would not feel the hollow place in her chest (used to housing only scraps of tolerance and pity for her father) filling up with something warm, resembling worry and bordering on love. But she would definitely touch her father's arm, like this.

"David, listen. I think you are confused. I think we ought to go home now." David answered by grabbing hold of her wrist and petting her, as if she were a rabbit or other small, skittish creature. She had to take charge. She had to be firm with him.

"David, you are not feeling well, and we need to go home. It's going to be fine. You can pack your things or I can pack them for you. We need to leave in half an hour."

"Hold your horses there, kiddo," he said. This was not the way her father talked. He sounded like a bad actor. Frances began pulling gear out of her tent.

"David, please cooperate with me. We have to go."

David sighed, "But what about the others?"

"It's just you and me."

"No, the others," David said, "Adam and Alex. And your mother." He was looking at Frances, lost and pleading.

Frances wanted no part of this. Parents get old, or lame, or sick, or demented, so what? But she hadn't done all those years of exhausting emotional work for this. To have David relinquish his memory. It seemed awfully convenient, her father forgetting the truth and creating this vague and pleasant ending to take its place. And it wasn't fair. She wanted him to carry some of it, too.

It was all such a long time ago.

"The boys aren't here, David. Remember?" she said. "Neither is mom. It's fine for us to go."

For a moment, her father's eyes looked clear again, and Frances thought he might have returned to her. Then he laughed, "Don't be silly, Frannie! They have to be around here somewhere."

"Wait right here, David. Will you please?" Frances quickly packed her father's things. They were of no use and made no sense: a stained dress shirt and tie, a Ziploc bag full of pens, and a carton of sour yogurt. Through the tent door, Frances could see him, sitting there, waiting for a family that would never come.

"It's time, David," she said, when she was through. "It's time to go home now." He looked frightened.

"But what about the rest of the family, Frannie? We can't just leave them behind."

Frances had no allies here, but worse yet, no witnesses. She had no idea what a good daughter would say, but she was all her father had.

"It's alright, David," she lied, "they are waiting for us at home."

And she wondered if she might not take it, too—if one day she found her own short cut to happiness. Frances knew, for now at least, she would accompany him.

WHY NOT TELL THE GIRL THE TRUTH?

Every Christmas Eve, Annie's extended family gathered to eat and exchange inexpensive gifts. They pretended that time and distance and small betrayals could be overcome with roast turkey, and chardonnay, and the force of a gathering of wills. Annie had decided that it was time to invite William to her childhood home for their holiday dinner. It was a late Sunday morning in early November. She and William were still in bed.

"I accept," William said, "Maybe this means that you are finally falling in love with me."

"And if you pass the litmus test, I will know that you are certifiable like the rest of them, so we can get on with things."

"And if I fail?" he said. Annie saw now that William felt unsure and wanted her to hear it. She was beginning to recognize when he shifted their banter toward something more. This happened frequently with William, and Annie did not always choose to join him.

She rested her head on William's stomach, her favorite spot, and he began to touch her hair. Annie told him, "Don't worry, they will love you." Now it was her turn to shift him, "but you should know something."

William was right there with her, "What's that?"

"It's not true what they say. About women eventually becoming their mothers?"

"I know," he said.

Annie lifted herself up onto her elbow, took in William's face. It was a nice face.

"And there are plastic animals grazing on the front lawn." William laughed. He was waiting for something more.

"Year *round*," she told him.

"That sounds like a forgivable Midwestern offense to me."

Annie didn't say anything. William's parents were Agnostic. He was originally from Portland—what did he know? He was in Chicago now, though, where at the age of thirty-eight Annie had miraculously found him at a friend's dinner party. Six months later, they moved into an apartment together near Wrigley Field. William taught undergraduate Sociology at DePaul University and he had warned Annie that this gave him an unfair advantage in all of his relationships. Annie knew that William was a man worthy of her admiration, but he required a great deal of her.

Annie still took photographs of small appliances for a living. This was supposed to have been temporary. She often said that she was lucky to work in her field. Privately, Annie had cataloged her favorite images of William. Baking bread. Reading the paper with Delilah the cat on his lap. Early one morning, when he thought that she was still sleeping, sorting his change on a sock so as not to make any noise. William was like this—generous, patient—in every endeavor. He was so kind to her, even when she was awful. Annie wasn't sure they would last.

Christmas Eve morning, Annie watched William clip his toenails over the toilet bowl. She had explained her family members to him in the weeks leading up to today. One trick was to keep the conversation light and the glasses full. Something occurred to her.

"You probably shouldn't say anything about not drinking." William paused at his big toe.

"What?" This was new to him.

"I mean, just let them pour you some wine. Don't make an issue of it."

"Annie, that's ridiculous," William resumed clipping.

It would take Annie years to explain the rules to William, and their train was leaving in two hours, "I know, I know. It's completely insane. You'll do it, though?"

"You can't be serious," he said, reaching for her. William was right, of course. Annie couldn't ask him to be someone he was not.

"God, William, I am reverting, aren't I? Forget it, forget I said that."

"Listen, I promise to be charming and gracious," he said, "and you must swear to regain your senses at the stroke of midnight." Annie kissed him hard on the mouth.

They had just an hour-long ride to Naperville. Annie conducted a final review of the entire clan with William, using the familial titles she had invented over the years. Grandmother Sigrid was her mother's mother, nearly blind, and they picked her up from St. Patrick's Residence for the Aged and Infirm only on special occasions. Grandmother Sigrid was a Catholic convert, and therefore a zealot of the most persistent sort.

"She sounds feisty," William said. Annie considered his assessment.

"You know what? That's absolutely true."

"How's this?" William cleared his throat, "'Lord, May I see thee today and every day in the person of the aged and sick.'" Annie laughed.

"Oh, that's good! Are you quoting scripture at me? That would go over quite nicely. Definitely keep that up."

"No, that's Mother Angeline Teresa. She's a Carmelite Sister. I teach her in my 'Death and Dying' class."

"Well, I don't know about that. You might as well pass it off as scripture. I doubt if anyone would know."

Then Annie explained, again, how Mother and Father did not like each other anymore and seemed to have forgotten why they ever had.

"And they've been together how long?" William asked. Annie had to think about it.

"It must be nearly forty-five years."

"I wonder why?"

"Exactly! That is my pervasive question. They really should have parted ways long ago."

"No, that's not what I meant at all. I wonder why they don't like each other anymore. I wonder what happened to them."

Annie hadn't wondered about her parents' unhappy marriage since she was a little girl. It was simply their condition. But William's question made her feel small. Sometimes she found herself growing angry with William for his incessant virtue, and then with herself, for her lack of it.

"Oh, who knows? But remember, when we get there—no questions about the girl."

"That would be Rebecca. Your brother Daniel's daughter," William said. He seemed pleased that he had this right.

"Close. I call him *Brother* Daniel. But not to his face."

"*Brother* Daniel, right. He's older than you. Harmless enough. You tolerate him. How does he feel about you? Do you know?"

Annie thought of her brother. (He was Danny to her once.) She considered the way the years had aligned him with their mother, her with their father.

"I imagine that the feeling is mutual," she said.

Brother Daniel was guilty of forcing his daughter—such a temperamental girl!—to come along to family gatherings a few times every year. When people were watching her, the girl ate. But only pickles and celery. All the girl ever drank was *Diet Coke.*

William asked, "So, what's the girl so furious about?"

"We think she's just making a scene," Annie told him.

"So, it's 'we' now, is it? You're a part of 'them' after all?" William was being playful, teasing Annie while gesturing toward an opening, if she'd take it. But Annie felt caught in an actual misstep, chided. She had to force a smile. William seemed to notice even this. He took Annie's hand, gave it a squeeze.

"So, do you like the girl?"

Annie hadn't thought about her niece in those terms. This train ride was exhausting. When had she last tried to engage the girl? She could not recall a time.

"Well, she's not easy to like, William. The girl is vapid. She admires those self-appointed celebrities who carry well-dressed infants and toddlers around like the latest designer handbags."

William laughed, "Who does that?"

William did not look at magazines in waiting rooms or watch commercial television. Annie found this limiting. "Never mind."

Next, William and Annie went over her sister-in-law, Tina. Tina, who tried to be a good mother to the girl, who frequently colored her hair at home, whose name suited her. She was a small and modest woman. Because there was no blood between them, Annie liked Tina the best.

"Right. I think I'll like her, too," William said.

"Don't get too excited," Annie told him, "Tina's not like us."

"Annie, come on. Are you kidding?"

Annie was growing tired of William's relentless goodness. "God, William. You know what I mean. Don't pretend that you don't."

"What? She's not white, not middle class, not educated? I wish I could play this back for you in a few days, Annie. I don't think you'd like what you heard."

"You know this is not about race or class. Don't paint me that way. And I'm sorry, William, but it's true. I'm not trying to be unkind. I'm just preparing you. None of them are like us." He would see.

They were almost done, and the train was almost there. Aunt Karen was coming. She particularly enjoyed explaining her recent gastric bypass surgery and showing the folds of loose skin that she hoped to soon have removed. (William cracked a smile, at least.) Aunt Karen was divorced and dating now, but would not be bringing a guest. Aunt Karen's gay son might be joining them later, for dessert and coffee. He recently become engaged to a toothy girl he met while teaching fourth grade at a private Christian elementary school. Obviously, the fiancé would come along, too.

"Wait now, how do we know that he's gay?"

Annie had known the gay son, her cousin, his whole life. William was still waiting, as if longevity were not sufficient proof.

"Fine, William. He told me so, OK? Well, the first time was when we were kids, before either of us really understood much about sex. Later, when we were both in college, he joined this angry fundamentalist church. So I asked him. He said yes, but that he only used to be gay. He had made a conscious decision to renounce the homosexual lifestyle."

"He actually said that?"

"Yes! I'm trying to tell you."

"Does Aunt Karen know?"

"Oh, I don't think so. But, isn't it awful? She's his mother."

"It's terribly sad."

"Thank you, William. You are finally catching on."

"Well, Aunt Karen might know. You've never said anything to her?"

"God, no! That woman needs a grandchild."

"Annie, quit it, will you?"

Annie knew that William was a good person, a much better person than she would ever be. She tried to slow her mind down. To listen to him.

"I'm being awful, aren't I?"

"I'm not saying that. I'm just saying that Aunt Karen might know that her gay son is gay. Maybe she's not pleased that he's getting married—to a woman—after all. We really don't know."

Annie wouldn't blame Aunt Karen. Not for longing for a grandchild, anyway. Who couldn't use someone convenient and safe to
love? William's version was more complicated, but hopeful. Annie
leaned her head against his shoulder. Sometimes if she let it, just
being with William softened her.

After Annie and William arrived, when the coats were piled on
the freshly made guest bed, the introductions were done, and drinks
were finally all around, Mother announced that Grandma Sigrid
had a curfew. Nine o'clock. Dinner would be in one hour, sharp.

They had all been visiting for about twenty minutes and Annie
was watching William. He looked so glad to be among them and she
saw him beginning to relax into himself. Father glanced down at
the glass of water in William's hand, "Say, you're not a recovering
something-or-another, are you?"

William looked at Annie, and she saw the kindness written on
his brow, saw him prepare to respond, when Mother interrupted,
"Don't be silly! Of course he's not. Now, I have an important job for
you, William."

Mother enjoyed giving instructions, particularly to men. She had
William fill the water goblets, and Annie offered to follow with a lemon
slice for each glass. Mother led the rest of the women into the kitchen,
and Father took Grandmother Sigrid to the living room. From the
dining room table, Annie could see Grandmother Sigrid being
stationed in a small but comfortable chair near the hearth. Father
was trying to start a fire, and Brother Daniel stood by ready to assist.

"This is nice," William said, "I feel like we're in an old movie."

Annie tossed a lemon slice at him. It landed on a china dinner
plate.

He picked it up and sucked on it, "You think I'm joking? This
is nice."

"Please, tell me that you're joking."

William poured water into another goblet. "No, I like them. So there." Annie imagined William infused with ready love and compassion. He seemed to tolerate everyone and everything. She wondered what this said about his unshakable affection toward her.

"Sigrid?!" Father was shouting at Grandmother Sigrid, "Sigrid?! Would you like some more ginger ale?!"

"In a little while," she said—and then, "For now, bring me just a tiny nip, just the tiniest nip-of-a-nip of brandy. But don't tell your wife. She's always been stingy."

Father winked at William as he passed on the way to the liquor cabinet, "Well, I aim to please."

Mother called out from the kitchen, "Annie? I could use your help in here!"

"Calling all vaginas," Annie whispered to William. He laughed.

"Honestly, do they need another one in there?" Annie worried about what Father and Brother Daniel might say to William. She worried about his quiet spirit among their frivolity.

"You'll be alright out here alone? I'm afraid that you'll have to make small talk with them. You know, or they'll accuse you of being too serious."

"Is this good?" William crossed his eyes. Then he pointed to the kitchen door, "Get! Get where you belong, woman." Annie laughed.

Mother and Tina were standing at the sink and counter at their respective tasks. Tina's hair was a deep chestnut, and it suited her. Aunt Karen was sitting at the kitchen table arranging olives on a relish tray. The girl was reading a magazine. She really was beautiful, and much, much too thin.

Tina said, "Annie! He's a cutie! Kind of quiet, but such a cutie!" She was tearing at the lettuce.

"I completely agree," Annie said. Tina spoke like a child sometimes. Still, Annie reminded herself, Tina was earnest.

"What gives in Hollywood?" Annie asked the girl. Annie could at least try. Why not? When the girl raised her magazine, Annie saw that it was *The New Yorker*. So, the girl could read. "Sorry about that," Annie said, "Wrong coast."

"No problem," the girl went back to her page.

"I have to confess, ladies, I just don't understand those comics," Tina said.

"It's not you. They're deliberately esoteric," Aunt Karen said, "to shut people like us out."

Tina seemed pleased, "Well, Rebecca asked for a subscription for her birthday this year. That was number one on her list! She likes culture. Art and things. But, she doesn't get those brains from me, I'm sure."

"It's a fine magazine," Annie said. And who knew? Maybe she and the girl would have things to talk about one day after all.

"You needed some help, Mother?" Annie asked. Though she suspected that she had really been summoned to field questions about William.

"Yes. No one in this room knows a thing about gravy. The drippings are on the stove. Can you start it, please?"

Annie hated gravy—the thick taste, the dull smell—but she had learned how to make it once, and so it had become her job. She turned the burner on, and began to stir at the grease in the frying pan. She knew to watch for just the right moment to add some water, flour, pepper, salt.

"Now, tell us all. How did you meet William?" Tina asked. And here it was.

"At a mutual friend's dinner party."

The girl stopped reading. She looked up at Annie, "Why do people say 'dinner *party*' anyway? What makes it a dinner party, and not just dinner?"

The girl was sincere, and the women were astonished. For the last several years, the girl had spoken to adults monosyllabically. They bore the weight of the moment.

"Well," Tina said, "a dinner party is different."

"I'm not asking *you*, mom. I'm asking Aunt Annie. *She* knows."

Annie felt, at once, flattered by the girl's new attention and a shoring up of her allegiance to Tina. Annie looked to Tina for something like permission. For the first time, she noticed the extra shadows under Tina's eyes. Of course, Tina was aging, just like the rest of them. But they could not risk losing the girl. A small shift, and Annie felt Tina entrusting the girl to her care in this moment.

"Yes, that's a good idea," Tina said, "tell us, Annie."

Annie smiled at Tina. "Well, this is a dinner party, I suppose. We've all been invited. It's polite to bring a little gift for the host. And I brought a guest."

Mother broke in, "All that, and they're a lot of work for the women. Annie, the gravy?"

"Right," Annie said. She gave it a quick stir and it was fine.

"That's *it*?" the girl said, "Is that *all*?" Annie recognized in the girl a grave and ardent desire for another life, a familiar longing that had once belonged to her as well. Tina was looking to Annie, stranded. But Annie had nothing else to give the girl. What else was there?

Remarkably, Aunt Karen spoke-up, "Of course that's not all! Not even close. At a real dinner party, you choose your own company. You serve whatever you like to eat, or what your friends do at least. And anything can happen."

"That's not true," the girl said. "About anything happening." But she was still talking, still listening.

"You asked a question and I'm telling you the truth. Treaties have been signed, movie stars discovered, people have died, all at dinner parties. You drink, you argue, you choke on a bone, who knows? Annie, that's where you met the love of your life, right? At a dinner party."

"Well, I am not sure that I would call him *that*," Annie said.

"Why not?" the girl asked, "What's wrong with him?" How had this all come back to her, and to William?

"Well, for one thing he's sullen," Mother said, "And dinner is in five minutes. How's that gravy coming, Annie?"

"He's not sullen, Mother. He's just—thoughtful," Annie said. Mother handed her the gravy boat and ladle.

"Well, I'm not privy to his heart, Annie. It's that face I'm worried about." Annie put some aluminum foil over the gravy boat to keep it warm. "But it figures. You always did like the brooders, remember?"

Annie thought of all the boys that she had cared for, all the men. The way her mother had helped her dismantle each of them, one by one.

The women were all looking at her, here in this kitchen. Annie saw the chrome toaster, the chrome blender, the chrome food processor. Everything matched. The light was perfect. Mother turned to verify dishes and trays and serving utensils. But Tina and Aunt Karen and the girl were all leaning toward her, their faces open and bright, like children hoping for something extraordinary.

Annie considered the prospect of an unencumbered love. There was Tina, subversively loving Rebecca—even as the girl pushed her away. And Aunt Karen, who had found some words for the girl, morsels for her starving frame. Aunt Karen, who at this moment might be wishing for her son a happiness that she didn't understand.

Annie liked William's ideas. His furrowed brow. His heart. Annie saw the girl—watching her.

"What's wrong with him Annie?" the girl asked again.

"I like his face," Annie told them, "And we make each other laugh."

"Oh, laughter! That's wonderful," Aunt Karen said.

"It is?" the girl asked.

"Oh, for heaven's sake, let's *eat*," Mother said, "Tell the others, will you, Tina?"

The women collected what they needed and carried everything into the dining room.

"You listen to me, young lady," Aunt Karen would not be stopped, "laughter is just as important as sex."

The girl laughed. Annie nodded. Yes, it was! They were all gathered now.

"Karen!" Mother said.

"Please, you think Rebecca doesn't know about sex?"

At this, Grandmother Sigrid said: "Ha!" And William smiled at Annie. *See? Feisty.*

Grandmother Sigrid was rosy with brandy and fire, and Daniel pulled a chair out for her. Mother and Father went to their spots at the far ends of the table. Tina sat down next to Father, Brother Daniel next to Mother. The girl took the place beside Aunt Karen.

William raised his eyebrows at Annie. She knew exactly what he was asking. Where to sit? There were a few extra chairs and settings, just in case. But who else was coming? Wasn't that just for dessert?

Annie would join William. She didn't care where. There was plenty of room, and they would all find their place.

SOME GOOD NEWS TO TELL

Margie unlocked the door to the Clothes Depot every Saturday morning at six. She had her keys, her Stanley thermos full of black coffee, her back pillow, and her egg salad sandwich. Some laundromats were open twenty-four hours these days, but the absentee owner of the Clothes Depot told Margie that trend would come and go. (His laundromat was staffed by experienced individuals, such as herself, and what kind of riffraff did laundry at two in the morning anyway?)

She flipped the switch and waited as the lights high above her warmed up, flickered, and then buzzed completely on. The one farthest to the back flickered, just a little, all day long. Regular customers avoided those machines because you couldn't always tell your whites from your lights, and you might end up with dingy tube socks when you were done for the day. Margie always seemed to forget to tell the owner about this problem during their weekly telephone conversations; he spoke too quickly, and Margie mostly tried to remember to breathe.

The older customers came before eight to get the best machines. They knew her by name and she knew them by their laundry soap, their machines, and their secrets.

"Morning Margie," said the man with one arm. Margie imagined he was a war hero, and treated him with respect.

"Morning yourself," she said. "Need change today, then?" He never did, and with his mesh bag draped across his good arm, he shuffled to the soap dispenser, which leaned against the pale-green plaster walls that surrounded them. He braced his bag of clothes against his hip and retrieved a miniature box of "Tide" from the machine. After starting his first load, he reached for the blue and yellow parakeet in his front coat pocket, and placed it carefully on the shoulder above his missing arm.

"Nice birdie," he told the parakeet, "Nice, nice birdie."

Margie took in the beginning of the tart, damp scent that would soon fill the place; by mid-afternoon it would numb her taste buds completely. She noticed that the evening attendant hadn't bothered to clean up after his shift. She did not remember this new kid's name. The turnover is terrible, the owner told her. Thank God he could count on reliable people, such as herself. Margie had missed just one week in the past seven years, and that was for her bunions. She worked clockwise around the floor and gathered a half-empty bottle of pop, a candy wrapper, two crushed packets of cigarettes, and a ribbed condom—which she quickly folded into the candy wrapper, glancing sideways at the man with one arm. He was talking to his parakeet, and saw nothing.

Next came the woman in galoshes. It was a quarter after eight, and she was late. Margie clenched her teeth as she saw the woman approach, but forgave her when she placed a chocolate doughnut on Margie's table.

"I brought you some breakfast, Margie," she said. "That coffee's ruining your teeth and your stomach lining. You have got to eat. Our bones aren't what they used to be when we were young, you know."

"Thanks," Margie answered, running her index finger along her upper front teeth, and reaching for the doughnut with the other hand.

The woman in galoshes looked pleased to find her section still available, despite her tardiness, and claimed her space by spreading her dirty clothes across two machines and one dryer. She went out-

side to her car and returned with another basket. She always came
with her own bottle of All.

When the morning sun reached the middle of Margie's table,
she twisted the lid off her thermos until it sounded a familiar hollow pop, and she filled her cup slowly, willing her right hand to stop
shaking. At ten minutes past nine, a wrinkled looking girl held the
door open with her foot and dragged in a basket filled with pajamas,
blue jeans, pastel brassieres, and a boy who appeared to be about two
years old. He held a turkey baster in his hand.

"Hey there," the girl said to Margie.

She was new and breezy, so Margie just nodded toward her, but
looked at the boy. He was using the turkey baster to lift his mother's
brassieres onto the gritty floor. (Good thing they weren't washed yet.)

"Cut that out," warned the girl, "or I'll take away your baster."

The boy looked up at her, and held tight to the kitchen utensil.
The girl lifted him onto a washer, and before sorting by color or del-
icacy, dumped half her basket into a machine. Margie was intrigued,
and so was the man with one arm, whose machines were across from
the ones the girl had claimed. She seemed unaware of the fact that
her laundering techniques were being watched and judged, and that
should she return, she might thereafter be known as the girl with
the boy with the baster, who doesn't use soap.

She looked about seventeen in the face, and Margie felt something sudden and strange toward the girl. She looked just like Clara.
Clara, Margie's oldest sister. Clara, easy to laugh. Clara, who took
the bus to San Diego one September day and never came home
again. Margie began to count the change, and make her piles of
paper and coins.

The girl found, at the bottom of her basket, a small box of Dreft
wrapped in plastic. Margie recognized it as one of those free sam-
ples that occasionally comes with a Sunday paper, or rarely, in the
mail like a gift. Margie decided that the girl was resourceful, but
unlearned, as she watched her sprinkle dry powder over the clothes.

"They'll spot if you do it that a way, Miss," cautioned the man with one arm.

The girl looked puzzled, and Margie felt herself want to grin. Rookie.

"You got to let the water fill up first. The soap'll just clump all up in there, see?" he explained.

"Oh, sure," the girl said. "It doesn't much matter, but thanks anyway. For the help, I mean."

She set the boy beside her and reached for one of the magazines provided courtesy of the Clothes Depot. Margie had read every one. It was a *Ladies' Home Journal* from 1988, and had a young Valerie Berti-nelli on the cover. The woman in galoshes said she had subscribed to the *Ladies' Home Journal* for the past nine years, and distinctly remembered her first issue.

The boy now stood in front of the man with one arm and stared at the parakeet seated on his shoulder. He pointed at the bird and said, "Da!"

"You like Birdie, do you?" the man said as the bird stepped lightly onto his finger, and he presented it to the boy, who took a large step back.

He had noticed the man's missing arm, again pointed and said "Da?"

Margie watched the man's face; he did not seem offended, but almost grateful. Who else but a child could ask about the arm? It had never occurred to her, and she had always tried to avoid looking at the stump or into the man's eyes, so as not to be discovered wondering. The parakeet safe on his shoulder-perch, the man folded his sleeve back to show the boy where his stump ended.

"I lost my arm, see? It got caught in the motor of a boat. It don't hurt me none, no more," he told the boy. I'll be damned. Margie felt betrayed. He was no war hero. He just had poor balance.

The boy pointed at the parakeet. "More," he said.

"That issue's got a good remedy for headaches," the woman in galoshes told the girl.

The girl flipped to the front cover and read out loud, "Home Headache Help," then flipped back to her spot. "I'll check that out," she said. But the girl just continued to slowly page through each glossy advertisement and article.

"Personally," the woman said, "personally, I haven't had a headache in fifteen years." The girl looked at the woman blankly, seemed to do some mental calculations, and then nodded at her with the admiration granted only to those who have earned it through the simple endurance of more years than one can imagine. A young bank teller had looked at Margie that way once, after they had discussed her long battle with the bunions.

"Hey," the girl said abruptly, "quit bothering that man."

"He's no bother, Miss," said the man with one arm. "We're just talking to Birdie here, right?"

"Birdie here. Birdie here," the boy repeated, touching her back gently with one finger, exactly as the man had shown him.

The girl turned her attention back to her magazine, and the woman in galoshes sat down next to her.

"Is that your boy? I mean, you're his mother, not a babysitter or something?" she asked.

Margie checked the time.

The girl exhaled a laugh, "Babysitter? No. I'm his mother, and we never had a babysitter, lady."

The woman in galoshes had two of her own children, three grandchildren, and a dead husband, God rest his soul. Margie often heard the woman complain that her daughter called every day, breathless with her troubles. Her son, though, was worse yet. He was a "little on the wild side," lived in Los Angeles and wrote rare, confusing letters on yellow legal paper. Sometimes, he even forgot to sign them. Every other Mother's Day or birthday she'd receive a dramatic flower arrangement, three or four days late, with a card signed by the florist—in a legible hand, at least, which was more than she could say for her son. Margie wondered which child she would choose for herself, the daughter, a hole she would never stop trying to fill, or the son, a gift that might never come.

The woman in galoshes said, "I could watch the boy for a bit. I'd enjoy it, really. And you could do an errand or two."

The girl looked at Margie now, as if for permission, studied the woman for a moment, and slipped her hand into her front jeans pocket. She found three dollars and some change.

"Oh no, don't pay me a thing. My grandchildren are worlds away. Truly now," the woman insisted.

"Well, thanks a lot. It's real good of you." The girl waved her boy over. "Hey, you listen to this nice lady. Help her with her clothes and things. I'll be back in a while," she rubbed the top of his head. "Half hour?" she asked the woman in galoshes.

"Sure. I've got a full load left," she told the girl.

The boy had wandered back to the man with one arm and the parakeet, and the woman in galoshes spoke in confidence to Margie as she transferred her clothes and began her last load. "Poor thing," she said. "Alone, raising a boy, and so young."

"There's worse things," Margie answered.

"Well, yes, there are," the woman in galoshes said, and then began a list of many worse things, borrowing troubles from her neighbor, her husband, God rest his soul, and her daughter.

At eleven, it was time for Margie to eat her sandwich. She folded the plastic wrap into a small square and placed it back into the brown bag. The man with one arm waved as he left. Margie waved back, finished her sandwich, and began to read a newer issue of *Show Dog World*.

A dryer buzzer sounded as the girl returned, carrying a small gourmet coffee from a shop at the end of the street. "Man, was that ever nice," she told the woman in galoshes. "Thanks again, lady."

The woman in galoshes just smiled and said, "It was nothing. He sure got on with our friend, here," and she turned to the empty chair where the man with one arm was supposed to be.

"He left ten minutes ago," Margie told her.

The girl looked over the center row of machines for her boy. She walked to the other side of the Clothes Depot and looked under an old table. "He likes to hide sometimes," she explained.

The woman in galoshes followed her, saying helpless things like: "He was just here," and "Oh dear. Oh dear."

Margie thought about the man with one arm, gently holding his bird. She imagined the woman in galoshes answering her phone later that afternoon, her anger and relief at the sound of her daughter's voice. Margie did not want to remember, this thing a person feels for another, if they are both lucky and brave; this complicated thing they only know to call love, closest to knowing and being known.

"He could have gone outside to the parking lot," Margie said, and went out to look. It was the only the second time she had ever left the building during her shift. Once, there had been a dryer fire. She checked the alley. The bus stop. The hair salon next door. When she returned, the two looked at her, but she only shook her head.

"You don't think someone could have come and well, I mean..." said the woman in galoshes. Margie willed the woman to keep those thoughts to herself.

The girl was awake now, fueled by coffee and fear. She ignored the woman's comments, and called the boy's name: "Jamie? Jamie! Are you in here? Are you hiding? Come here. Right now. I mean it!" Nothing. Margie remembered the squirrels in winter, and began opening every dryer door.

"Oh, my, Lord," whispered the woman in galoshes. "I'll never forgive myself."

Every slam of a door sounded a definitive no.

Then, curled inside the farthest oversized dryer, there he was.

"Here's your boy," Margie told the girl and then watched as the girl took the boy into her arms.

"Birdie, Birdie," the boy told his mother, and reached up to touch her cheek with his finger.

Margie looked on as the girl gathered the boy in again, and rocked him, and held his body against her own.

BUT I WILL TELL YOU OTHERWISE

You may hear that it came to no good when Cha Cha McGee moved to town, but I will tell you otherwise. I still reside in the same narrow place, and though it's been close to thirty years since I last saw Cha Cha, I still remember the first time she invited me inside. My aunt had sent me over with a blueberry pie. Cha Cha came to the door in bare feet and a yellow babydoll negligee, two perfect round peaches where I kept my secret raisins. Her family was new, and she was one grade ahead of me in school. I had seen her there a few times, but I had no idea what Cha Cha McGee was made of yet. She just stood there, looking at me through the screen door.

"It's Janie Jameson," I told her.

"Hey," she said.

"My aunt Sarah made this for you," I held up the pie.

"Who the hell's that?" Cha Cha asked me.

I wasn't used to girls swearing. And I wasn't used to explaining anything about my family. I don't think I ever had cause to tell anyone the story, not before Cha Cha McGee. Everyone already knew that the day before I turned eleven my parents and brother had driven off the high bridge by mistake. Cha Cha listened, and I ended with the fact that now I had to live with my aunt, Sarah Jameson.

"Oh," she said, "Well, that makes sense." It was such a strange response, and she was still just standing there looking at me. I thought maybe she was slow.

"The pie's a welcoming gift," I said, "for your family." I was raised to have good manners, brought up to be kind. For so many years, even later as a woman and a lover, I thought that being kind meant doing things I didn't want to do so as not to hurt someone else's feelings. I wanted Cha Cha to take that pie from me so that I could go home, but she had already decided that I should stay.

"Well, Janie Jameson," she said, except it sounded like an accusation, "are you coming in or not?" I stepped into the McGee's dark kitchen, stood there until Cha Cha said, "Sit down, why don't you?"

She placed the pie on top of my Aunt Sarah's good cotton dishtowel, in the middle of the kitchen table. Cha Cha hadn't even said anything about the pie yet. Not thank you, or it looks wonderful, or how nice. I wanted a witness. For someone with good sense and authority to see that pie. I wanted to teach Cha Cha something about how we did things. "Are Mr. and Mrs. McGee around?" I asked.

"Momma's asleep and so are the twin babies. And Mr. McGee?" she laughed at this, "he's already down at Reuben's. Can you believe that?" Cha Cha laughed again. I assumed it was about mothers who slept the afternoon away, and fathers drinking hard before supper.

The year before I might have laughed right along with her. I used to laugh like a regular girl. But I was still sad and too young and hadn't made any sense of losing my family. I could have pretended to laugh. I had learned how to do that. From the start, something about Cha Cha McGee made me want to tell the truth. So I told her that I wasn't that particular anymore, that even a lazy mother and a drunken father sounded pretty good to me.

For the first time of many, Cha Cha McGee gave me something unexpected and completely necessary. "Listen," she leaned in, whispering, "he's not my real daddy, you know. He's not even married to my momma. And he's not her first boyfriend like that, either. He only talks to me when he wants something. The twin boys are his own, but not me."

"Oh," I said. I was both uncertain and grateful regarding what I would later come to understand as her peculiar brand of kindness.

Then she put on some coffee for us, which I didn't care for yet. But I was beginning to like her company.

"Make mine with milk and sugar," I told her. And Cha Cha McGee laughed at this. Oh, her laugh was a singular sound.

"Why bother? I always take mine black. Say! Blueberry pie's always better when it's fresh, don't you think?" Cha Cha said. I could feel how clever she was, where this was going. I wasn't sure I wanted to stay anymore, but I wanted to see what Cha Cha would do next.

"Yes," I told her.

"We'll have some of this pie to go with our coffee, then." She got up to get a knife. I was worried that no one in charge had seen the pie yet, not knowing that most of the time, Cha Cha McGee was the one in charge.

"We should wait," I said, "because it's supposed to be for all of you." She was already cutting the first piece. "That's why my aunt sent it over!"

"Nice of her," Cha Cha said. She placed the piece of blueberry pie on a chipped saucer rimmed with tiny pink flowers and tiny green leaves, and then she pushed it across the table at me, "Company first."

From that moment, I knew that it would never be easy to say no to Cha Cha McGee. We ate those first pieces of pie quickly, without talking. She crossed her legs at her ankles, the way my Aunt Sarah said a lady should while wearing a dress. And even though Cha Cha was in a nightie, and I was wearing blue jeans and my Peter Pan blouse, I crossed my ankles, too. Then we sipped our coffee and talked for a while like this was our common way.

When her piece was gone, Cha Cha said, "You be sure to tell your aunt that the McGees enjoyed her blueberry pie." She was running her index finger across flowers and leaves, sucking off the blue.

"I will," I said and stood up to go. But Cha Cha wasn't through with me yet.

"Janie Jameson, didn't your folks ever teach you any manners before they passed?" That stopped me. Here she was, speaking of my dead parents so easy, when no one else would say a word. At the time, I didn't know the value of candor, the varying shades of integrity or why Cha Cha's way could feel so much better than anything I had ever known before.

And after a while, Cha Cha said, "I don't suppose anyone will miss this." She lifted out another piece of blueberry pie and put it in front of me. "And I'll have another myself." This time, she tipped the whole pie plate toward her and pulled almost a quarter of it out onto her own saucer.

"Cha Cha McGee," I whispered, but I was impressed. "There'll be none of it left!"

"You're right, Janie!" she feigned surprised. She was a fine actress, already. "Well then, we may as well send this plate home with you clean!" Then she gave me a wink. "More coffee?"

I knew right then that Cha Cha McGee was what people would call trouble. And I knew that I wanted to be her friend.

"Just a little," I said.

Looking back, I don't suppose I've ever loved anyone as much as I loved Cha Cha McGee. She was my first real friend and together we crossed the perilous bridge that spans being a girl and being a woman. Who can travel this alone? No one should have to. It is the most dangerous terrain. Cha Cha loved anything sweet and so almost every day after school we would walk to the store at the edge of town, just to get Cha Cha some candy. We always got two lollypops for the baby boys, too. Cha Cha said she didn't care that the twins were half Mr. McGee's—they couldn't help that. She would make damn sure that they grew up to be good anyway. On our walks to the Candy Pantry, Cha Cha taught me many things: how to pull the bottom of my shirt up and through my collar, halter-style, so that my soft belly showed; how to swing my hips side to side, just enough, as I moved. I pretended to be brave, and for a time I was. Now I know that I was simply lucky. Too many girls never get a chance to try their womanhood on, like a costume. Too few can claim their own season of such recklessness.

Another favorite pastime of Cha Cha McGee's involved standing in front of the Lady Pearson's house and imagining what went on inside. I did a lot of following Cha Cha around back then but I couldn't see what she found so fascinating about the Lady Pearson. I looked at the jars of colored water that the Lady Pearson had arranged on the old picnic table in her front yard. Most of us were afraid of the Lady Pearson. There were plenty of rumors about her. Depending on who you asked, she decorated the jars with rare wild flowers, or blood and guts.

One afternoon, standing there with Cha Cha looking at the jars, I was surprised by a memory of my mother. My mother had been sitting on the bathroom floor with a tiny dead baby in a white handkerchief on her lap. I was sorry for her, but to me it looked disposable—the bony, bloody slick of a hen's egg. (This had happened in the spring, before the high bridge.) My brother and I would have been seven and ten, respectively. After that, our mother couldn't seem to stop talking about the three other dead babies she had back when she was still a young wife. We could look them all up in the town hall, she told us. It was a matter of public record. Aunt Sarah started coming over most evenings to make us dinner, and when our mother remembered to tuck us in and kiss us goodnight, she would sing an odd song about meeting up one precious day with all her lost little souls.

I am thankful that as a child the possibility, the likelihood, never came to me in any concrete way: perhaps my mother meant to drive off the high bridge that day. And my father and brother happened to be, most unfortunately, along for the ride. But the recollection of my mother, there on the bathroom floor, was one seed of truth. I began to recognize the nature of my mother's irrevocable, terminal sadness. So in that first moment of remembering with Cha Cha, I'm sure that I missed my mother. But even more I was confused and inexplicably angry. I wanted to scare my friend. I wanted to mar something she admired, to shake her the way I so often felt shaken.

"You know," I told her, "they say that the Lady Pearson's got body parts in those jars."

Cha Cha looked at me hard. Then she turned to the jars, "That's a load of crap," she said, "They're pretty."

How I had wanted to take it back, to tell Cha Cha I already knew that. I knew it long before her. The first beautiful thing I ever saw were the Lady Pearson's jars of colored water.

There came a time when Cha Cha grew to know the Lady Pearson very well, and so I knew her, too. Some of the worst stories about town weren't true after all, but the Lady Pearson kept a better secret of her own. Cha Cha and I had not yet heard the real story from anyone. (And I never did hear it, directly, from anyone but her.) To speak it: to say that the Lady Pearson had once been the local whore, was also to say that there had been patrons in our town. Who would they be? Our banker, our doctor, our mayor. (Our fathers, our husbands!) Who else? The Lady Pearson told us that she knew exactly which men had fallen over the years. She kept a journal. But she did not name names. She did say that these were the men of our town, where she herself had been born and most certainly would die. Sometimes she liked to imagine them all back, she told us, long ago, when they were just still boys and girls just like Cha Cha and me.

I imagine the scene, too. There they sat, hands scrubbed, around the dinner table waiting for Daddy. The buttered potatoes congealed and mother nipped at the drink she had prepared for her husband, a taste she might soon acquire for herself. In walked Daddy, rumpled and flushed, forty-five minutes past due. Famished and reeking of her. If those boys and girls, most of them grown up now into husbands and wives themselves, had witnessed the exchange of looks, words, accusations, denials, most had forgotten, as children conveniently do. They preferred to remember their fathers as providers and righteous men. Those who could not avoid recalling their fathers' indiscretions simply created other reasons to hate the Lady Pearson.

A smart woman who knows her own pleasure in a town full of foolish men and frigid women is necessarily under great suspicion. Such a woman is thought either a witch or a bitch, and the Lady Pearson was frequently called both. The Lady Pearson didn't often seem lonely, though, as she enjoyed the latest crevices of her own mind, and the company of fine music followed by conversation. She said that she relished the quiet as well, for it never seemed empty to her.

And I must agree with her there. The longer I remain unmarried though seldom alone—and when alone, seldom unhappy—the more it seems that I risk a fate like that of the Lady Pearson. And the older I become, the better that sounds to me.

When I was a girl, my aunt Sarah and I attended services at the First Methodist Church of the Way. The McGee family never went to church, but Cha Cha used to warn me about some of us who did. The social hour that followed our church services is as close to the fires of Hell as I ever hope to get. I remember smallish boys and self-conscious girls from my seventh grade class standing around long brown tables eating cookies, drinking watered-down apple juice, and having nothing worthwhile to say.

Cha Cha had told me to watch out for my classmate Nancy Carpenter in particular. That was easy enough, as I had never really liked Nancy. She seemed too perfect, or was trying to be. I suspected that Nancy Carpenter hated Cha Cha because the boys preferred her to Nancy now. Cha Cha was never shy about how pretty she was, and she was smart, too.

I suppose Cha Cha was what so many boastful parents now like to call "gifted," although Cha Cha actually was. I never saw her study, though she loved to read anything and remembered every word. Our schoolwork was not rigorous in any way. The parents in our town were content with their children learning whatever academics, religion, and civics they had learned, and anything more would have been suspect. I was smart enough, but memorizing facts had always seemed challenge enough for me. Cha Cha was an inherently curious person, though, which was frowned upon in our school. She made no pretense of anything but the boredom and frustration she felt every day. There is such a thing, I'm sure, as a good teacher who fosters thinking and welcomes dissent, and perhaps even one who might be thrilled with (instead of threatened by) a student like Cha Cha McGee. But we had none of these.

I pointed out to Cha Cha that before she came to town, Nancy Carpenter had been the best student in school. How Cha Cha had quickly surprised everyone, including me, when she showed what she could do. Such as never missing a spelling word. Ever. Cha Cha said even so, I needed to be careful, too. She said that Nancy was full of spite, and claimed she could smell it on her.

So I couldn't wait to tell Cha Cha, when one Sunday Nancy proved her right, once again. Nancy Carpenter was loud, showy, an excellent liar.

"Janie, my Momma says it's real charitable, the way your aunt is looking after them McGee's," Nancy said. She knew that I had to smile and take it with all the witnesses. "Momma said you all been bringing them pies and what not, and if that isn't real good of you." I know plenty of women who once were girls like Nancy. They grow up to be the women who run things in order to gossip, and the ones who desperately work and spend in order to remain young for their husbands.

"Well, my Aunt Sarah's a real Christian after all," I told her.

"Momma thinks a good girl like you ought to watch herself though, Janie, running with that kind." Nancy's mother was the laziest teacher at our school and a terrible snoop.

"So what?" I said, and for emphasis took a bite of my peanut butter blossom cookie.

"That's just fine by me, Janie," Nancy said, easing herself into a grey folding chair. "But you know what they say? Birds of a feather."

Later I told Cha Cha that I didn't care to be classed in the same genus or species as Nancy Carpenter because I saw for myself what kind of creature she really was.

Sometimes, on our trips to the Candy Pantry, Cha Cha and I would climb over the chain link fence in the field behind school, and one Monday Cha Cha stopped.

"There's no park."

"What?"

"It's a stupid name for our school, Janie," Cha Cha told me. "Parkview." She was waiting for me to catch up in my mind. We both knew by now that Cha Cha McGee was faster than me, in every respect. "Get it? There's no park."

And she was right again, of course. Cha Cha always noticed things like that. When I told her how after Dutch Elm came through the Education Board had run out of money for new trees, she laughed for almost half a minute. Cha Cha said I was hilarious. She said that a lot but I was hardly ever joking. We were already halfway to the Candy Pantry when Bart Benson pulled up next to us in his truck.

"Hello Mr. Benson," I said, looking into the cab. The girls at school thought Bart Benson looked just like Burt Reynolds and he always seemed to have a brand-new truck. He was driving along slowly with us as we walked.

"Hey Janie," he said quickly, and then looked at Cha Cha. I was used to this. I didn't get much attention whenever Cha Cha was around, "You young ladies need a ride someplace? It's no trouble, you're both on my way."

Cha Cha stopped and so did the truck. She turned to meet Bart Benson eye to eye. Cha Cha McGee looked everyone in the eye when she talked, and as a girl I admired her for it. It's a skill I'm still working on. I remember the way Bart Benson smiled at Cha Cha as he reached over to open the door. I had known him all my life, but I had never seen that kind of smile before. I took a step forward, but Cha Cha put her arm out, blocking me.

"You can drive your truck straight to Hell," Cha Cha said to him. Then she took my hand and marched me away from the street. We were headed into someone's yard.

We could hear Bart Benson calling after us, "That's funny. You really think you're somebody special, don't you Cha Cha McGee? You really think you're somebody?"

"What are we doing?" I asked. Cha Cha was walking too fast, and her legs were much longer than mine.

"Short cut," she said.

"I'd rather get a ride!" I looked back. Bart Benson had laid on his horn once, and now was watching us go.

Cha Cha didn't turn around and she didn't slow down, "Janie, you don't know anything."

"Yes I do!" I said. She was only a year older than me, and I was growing tired of her acting so much wiser. "I know plenty."

"Not about assholes like Bart Benson," she said, her strides still rhythmic.

I thought I had her now.

"Well, I know him a lot better than you. Mr. Benson goes to my church." That just made her laugh.

"I don't care what that asshole does with himself on Sundays, Janie," she said. Then she stopped walking and looked at me softly, sad, like she was about to tell me something that might finally break my heart. "It's not the first time he's offered me a ride, okay? And I've gone with him, too."

"So?" I said. She sat down in the grass. I sat down next to her and we didn't say anything for a while. I had no idea what we were waiting for.

"We kissed a couple of times," she told me, "and other stuff." I didn't understand.

"But Cha Cha," I said, "Mr. Benson is a grown-up. And he's married."

"Janie, you're such a good girl." Cha Cha was a girl, too, and my friend, "Listen, he wouldn't take no for an answer. He's a bad man, Janie. And we have to stay away from him. Both of us." I thought she might be making it up. I wanted her to be making it up. I didn't know what to say. "Come on, it's time to go get ourselves something sweet."

Then Cha Cha stood up, and pulled me up with her. Cha Cha was only thirteen, but she seemed far older to me, now. I wasn't jealous anymore. And I was afraid for my friend. But I was too young and fortunate to fully understand precisely what was at stake for Cha Cha McGee.

Why does a man like Bart Benson, or any such man, lust after a young girl? I often wonder still, though it is not pleasant to consider. Maybe such a man did not mature past his boyish sticky dreams and acts of self-gratification. Maybe he was poked and stuck himself, as a boy, electing to forget in his mind, unable to do so in his groin, with his hands. The boy grows up, becomes a man, has children of his own, and should know better. He does know better. Isn't it nice to imagine castration would do the trick? I used to think so. It seems to me now, though, that this really is the least of it. Once such a man has been made, he would find a way.

Every night at ten, like clockwork, my Aunt Sarah fell asleep in the front room with a book across her chest. On clear nights when there was a moon, I snuck out through the back door and went to see Cha Cha McGee.

It was one of those nights, a Sunday, when everything changed. We sat on the roof like we always did, and Cha Cha told me about the way she had woken up in a quiet house. She poured a bowl of cereal, made herself some coffee and sat down in the stillness. Around lunch, she got a bad feeling. The last thing she wanted to do was wake

Mr. McGee while he was sleeping it off but the bad feeling was so strong she went upstairs anyway. And as soon as she opened the door to the room he and her mother shared, Cha Cha knew that they all had gone. Her mother had left the window wide open, Cha Cha said. This was just careless. She would never forgive her mother for that.

I remember thinking first about those sweet little boys with no more lollys and no more Cha Cha McGee to love them up. Then I thought of my friend, standing there alone and cold, at the top of the stairs.

"We need to build a bonfire," I said. Cha Cha looked at me in a brand new way. We took what was left of her mother, some fancy clothes Cha Cha never even saw her wear, a box of letters from old boyfriends, and some cologne. Cha Cha said she did not want to touch anything belonging to Mr. McGee, so I handled whatever he had left behind. We hauled everything out to the dirt driveway, poured her mother's cologne on top of the pile, and I lit a match.

"Jasmine," Cha Cha said, when the smoke reached up to us, and I agreed.

The fire burned too quick and hot. But it was beautiful, and Cha Cha and I had made it together, and I didn't want it to die. I threw on paper and trash, some sticks, anything I could find in the yard.

When the fire was low Cha Cha said, "Let's go in."

We sat down in the hall and Cha Cha pulled open a box with a few little shirts and pairs of pajamas. She was crying, but I knew that she would not want me to mention it, now or ever. She held up a baby shirt, "Don't worry, the twins won't need these. They barely even fit anymore."

"Can I keep something?" I said. She told me to have my pick.

Then we folded every tiny thing, dirty or fresh, all into nice tidy squares and placed them in the best drawer in the house.

Cha Cha said she'd had the whole day to think. She already had a plan and before she would tell me she made me sign in blood that I wouldn't tell a soul. Cha Cha McGee wasn't going anywhere. She was going to stay and raise herself alone, which we both acknowledged really wouldn't be such a change.

Cha Cha kept house and I kept my word, but after a while people started to notice. Cha Cha had always been thin, but she was starting to run out of food. The McGee's never had much in their pantry, and even though I gave Cha Cha everything I could, we didn't have much to spare at my house, either. Cha Cha's favorite little dress wasn't tight any more.

"Cha Cha McGee," Nancy Carpenter said in a whisper, loud though, so the rest of us could hear, "you wore that thing twice last week. What are you, some kind a prison-a-war? Are your people too poor to make gravy?"

"It's alright," Cha Cha whispered back, louder yet, "your asshole boyfriend likes me just fine." And it was true. All the boys liked whatever she wore. Especially that blue flowered sundress with straps as thin as sewing thread.

My Aunt Sarah worked at our school. She pulled the tables and chairs out for lunch, cleaned up, and put everything away again after. She watched me give my lunch to Cha Cha every day. She watched my friend fading away.

"Are her folks really that bad off?" she asked me, more than once. I would only shrug, my secret kept, and my loyalty to Cha Cha tested. But I couldn't save Cha Cha McGee in the way we had planned. After Aunt Sarah told the principal and the teachers that the McGee's must really in trouble, some of them went over before church one Sunday morning to find Cha Cha home alone. Yes, it was true. Her family had been gone for months and she didn't know where. Only one remarked on her fortitude, several her lies, and a few more on the filth. Aunt Sarah told me that Cha Cha McGee would have to become a ward of the state now.

"Cha Cha won't have to become a ward of the state," I said, "because she'll become my sister, instead. She's going to come and live with us." I suppose that I had convinced myself, with my young logic, that if I posed my greatest hope as a declaration rather than a question, my aunt would be unable to tell me "no."

"I was afraid of this, Janie," Aunt Sarah said, and I started to cry. "I'm so sorry." She tried to pull me close, but I wouldn't let her. "I know how fond you are of the girl, but we just can't."

"She's not just a girl," I said. "She's Cha Cha McGee. And she's my friend."

"I know, I know. I'm afraid Cha Cha McGee is too much of a handful for me."

I was offended now. It seemed to me that everyone, even my own aunt, thought Cha Cha McGee possessed something remarkable, extraordinary, that I couldn't identify and apparently lacked. "I'm a handful, too, and you took me in."

My aunt laughed at this notion, a quick release, "Oh, Janie. You're a very good girl. And you're my flesh and blood."

That night, I didn't bother with the moon and I didn't care if my Aunt Sarah heard me go out. I found Cha Cha up on her roof, waiting for me.

"They told me to be ready first thing in the morning. Damn it, Janie! I would have been fine, except for the food."

"I asked if you could come and live with us," I was ashamed of my aunt. "But she said no! I hate her. How could she say no?"

"It's not her, Janie," Cha Cha said. "It's everyone." And by this, even then, I knew exactly what she meant. It was awful, the way that the people and parts of our town, together, added up to something ugly.

"I'll just come with you, then," I told Cha Cha. "Wherever you go. We'll be like sisters."

"You can't, Janie," she said. In truth, I was both relieved and stricken. At that moment, Cha Cha McGee was more real to me than anyone. Just being near her made me real, too.

"The fools can tell me I'm off to the Children's Home, but they are quite mistaken."

"What do you mean?" I said. I didn't want to lose my friend. I was selfish, really, and didn't think about her fate. I was naïve enough to believe that Cha Cha McGee would be fine wherever she went. And I wanted to know exactly where to find her, "Please, don't run away."

"Janie, it's only called running away if you don't know where you're going." She had a bag already packed full of her things. She told me the Lady Pearson's house was just under two miles away. That night Cha Cha McGee would knock on the Lady Pearson's door and ask for the woman to take her in. I wouldn't let Cha Cha go there alone.

We were cutting through yards and dark streets, the way we knew how, when we saw the headlights of Bart Benson's truck pointing at us. He spotted us, stopped and got out. He was standing there in front of us, like a cowboy. He told us, now settle down girls. He said they had figured Cha Cha might try to run tonight, and he had volunteered to go and get her. I turned to Cha Cha for our next move, but she was just standing there, looking at Bart Benson.

He smiled and took a few steps forward. I remember wondering what was wrong with Cha Cha. Where was my friend with all her choice words?

"Cha Cha!" I shouted at her, to try and wake her up. We had to get away and she wasn't doing anything. I had no occasion as a reference point. Now, of course, I see how fortunate I was, that circumstance had given me no reason to understand how Cha Cha McGee must have felt at that moment as a girl, just a girl, facing off in the dark with man like Bart Benson.

"That's good," he said to Cha Cha. He was getting closer, looking at her skinny wrist, like he was sizing up whatever fight was left in her bones. "That's good," he told her. He said not to worry, that he knew the Director of the Children's Home quite well. The man was very fond of wayward tramps, like herself. Cha Cha McGee would never be lonely. "And you're cooperating. See? That's very good."

I felt an unprecedented surge of rage toward Bart Benson, a new and useful kind of hatred. Cha Cha McGee was there in the flesh, but the rest of her was going, going, gone. I have known times like this myself by now, of course, times of grief and shock. But that night I witnessed my friend's actual departure. I saw Cha Cha McGee's frightened spirit fly and leave her there, empty, to fend for her earthly self.

How could I have known that a girl who has been trained up, a girl who has nowhere else to go, will crawl in (again and again) next to the likes of Bart Benson? But I believe something in me must have understood the threat, even then. Something in me knew where Cha Cha McGee would be forced to land when she was ready to come back to her body.

I have never been bad, not really. And though I still couldn't bring myself to tell Bart Benson to go to Hell, I was ready to do my best to send him there. I looked at his truck: the driver's side door left open, the keys in the ignition, the engine running. We all knew how to drive back then. I didn't even close the door before I shifted into forward. Bart Benson turned his head just in time to see me hit him square in the face with the grill of his truck. The headlights were glaring at him, curling up in the road, gurgling his fury.

I shouted at Cha Cha, "Get in here!" And just like that, she was back. Cha Cha climbed over me, into the passenger seat, as I put the truck into reverse.

"Holy shit, holy shit! Look at what you did, Janie. Holy shit, look at what you did!"

"Cha Cha!" I said. I'm sure I reasoned that we had enough sins against us at that moment without unnecessary cursing.

"Janie, are you kidding me? You just hit Bart Benson with his truck, and you're after me about my language?" Now she was laughing. "You are so funny, you are so damn funny." My friend Cha Cha McGee was laughing, my favorite sound, and she couldn't stop and I started laughing, too. I turned left, heading toward the Lady

Pearson's house. Cha Cha was craning her neck back, trying to make something out through the cab window.

"Janie, he's barely moving. That's not good."

"Well, that's your opinion," I said. We were quiet then. I delivered Cha Cha to the curb in front of the Lady Pearson's house. We saw her standing in her doorway, waving, like she had been expecting us.

Cha Cha told me, "You really should come in. I bet she'll know what we should do."

No, I said. It was time to give Bart Benson back his truck.

How I imagined and did what came next is still a mystery to me. And it's been a secret that Cha Cha McGee and I have both kept all these years.

The road was nice and dark when I parked the truck right next to Bart Benson's body. I found a flashlight, a rag and a screwdriver in a toolbox in the back of the truck. The flashlight caught some blood on the shiny bumper, so I wiped it clean with the rag. Then I put the flashlight and the wrench near Bart's right hand. I took the screwdriver and punctured the tire closest to his body. He wasn't making sounds anymore, and I took that as a good sign.

I stood over Bart Benson then, trying to feel something acceptable. But I wasn't sorry Bart Benson was dead, or that I had been the one to make him so.

All this took me less than five minutes. I threw the screwdriver and rag into the woods on my way home.

That night I tried to fall asleep, but kept throwing up. I imagined this was my punishment and now there would be nothing left in me but secrets. I was getting a cold drink of water at the kitchen sink when my Aunt Sarah caught me and asked what I was doing awake at that hour.

"Just cleaning up," I said, rinsing out my glass.

"The dishes are done, Janie," she said. Then she saw my face, and asked me, "Are you sick?"

I said I didn't know, because I had never felt better or worse in my life.

She came to my side.

"Are you hot at all?" and she touched my forehead, "Oh, Janie. You are burning up!" Then Aunt Sarah put her cheek against mine, and that did me in.

She smelled just like pink soap, and my mother. I put my arms around her neck. Aunt Sarah knew about Cha Cha McGee without anywhere good to go, but I couldn't tell her about the Lady Pearson or Bart Benson, probably dead in the road. I couldn't tell her any of this. I couldn't—

"What are all those birds doing in here?"

"I'm calling the doctor right now," she said.

And then I was out.

I still remember my fever dreams. I started on the head of a pin, flew down the front hall stairs and out the screen door. I saw the whole town, all of it, and everyone. There was Parkview School and some boys smoking in the bare yard by the fence. There was Nancy Carpenter letting her boyfriend put his left hand up her shirt. Aunt Sarah was reading a book, Bart Benson was trying to start his truck, and five dead babies were stuffed into a grey filing cabinet at the town hall. And then those babies were floating in the Lady Pearson's jars of colored water. I could see each one of them, each with a jar of purple or red or blue. Because where else can you go when you are just a baby with a little fishy spine and all that original sin to carry around on your back? It was one last chance to be something beautiful.

I ran hot for three nights. After, everyone was still talking about Cha Cha McGee running away and poor Bart Benson killed, hit and run, while he was trying to change his tire. That all sounded close enough to me. For two weeks, I waited every day after school in front of the Lady Pearson's place, hoping for some sign of Cha Cha. I missed her, but I was careful not to give anything away. Finally, I saw Cha Cha coming out to the front yard, holding a metal watering can.

"Cha Cha McGee!" I called out, "There you are. Are you O.K.?"

"Of course I am. I just had to lie low until things passed, what do you think? I'm eating goat cheese and learning Latin. We're listening to Chopin." I didn't know Chopin then, and I didn't know what to say to my friend.

"But what are you doing with that watering can?" I shouted again. She began filling a jar with fresh purple.

"Quit yelling, will you?" she yelled back at me. Then, in the steady voice that I knew so well, "I can hear you fine, Janie. The Lady told me this water turns sour after a while, so I'm changing it." Cha Cha gave me a smile, a wink, and went back inside.

Sometimes I wonder about that moment still, what might have happened if I had followed Cha Cha McGee into that house. Would we have become like sisters? When it was my time, would I have found something extraordinary in me? Would I have gone away, like my friend—on to the University, to Europe and back, to the city, and a life I can only just imagine?

Cha Cha McGee showed up at Parkview School the next morning in a brand new red silk dress. The get-up, as the teachers called it, was completely inappropriate. The Lady Pearson sent Cha Cha with a typed letter officially declaring that Cha Cha McGee was her legal ward now. They had acquired all the necessary documentation from the state, and it was all a matter of public record.

"Cha Cha McPearson," Nancy Carpenter tried to rename her, but Cha Cha was already leaving us behind.

We all just looked on and on at Cha Cha McGee in that red silk dress, becoming as she was.

PLEASE TELL US YOUR BEAUTIFUL SECRET

The angel of death was running behind schedule. It had been an exhausting day, even for a celestial being.

Sister Josephine was playing Bach's "Prelude in D Minor" on her upright piano when the angel of death found her, so he knew that she must be expecting him.

When he had tried to take his previous client, Chuck Hauser, from his bed at hospice, Chuck had been reluctant to leave his wife behind. The angel of death pointed out the way his wife was stroking Chuck's hand, how she had loved him but would never be through loving him. The angel of death informed Chuck that his wife would remarry a good man, a widower with the children and grandchildren they had once wished for, that she would be happy again, in a different, less feverish way.

"Sorry I'm late," the angel of death told Sister Josephine now, just for his own entertainment. Everyone knew that adults could not hear angels while they were still alive, unlike dogs and unattended children.

"Yes," said Sister Josephine, "I am quite tired, actually."

The angel of death was shocked because this had never happened to him personally. Had not, as far as he knew, happened to any of them for several hundred years.

The angel of death composed himself. He was in charge here. And pronounced: "Sister Josephine, your time has come."

She smiled at him now (how lovely!) and stood up to reach for his hands.

"Is this alright?" she asked.

The angel of death honestly didn't know.

Her good nature unnerved him. Most were like Chuck Hauser, so the angel of death was used to selling. Good news! He had told Chuck only hours before, in just over nine years (which would seem a very short time to Chuck now that he was dead!) his wife would die, too! And so, the very best parts of them would indeed meet again. Chuck said forget it, he didn't believe in any of that crap. Eventually though, Chuck had ascended, spent but free.

But here, this Sister Josephine was surprising him again. The angel of death would win (he always did) and the end would be the same, so he took her hands in his own for the moment.

"Any questions?" he asked her, to be polite.

"Oh, yes!" Sister Josephine said, her feet already stepping out of her body, "I've been wondering for the longest time now, what is your name?"

In his entire service, the angel of death had never once been asked his name. He had to think about it, laughed when he remembered, and called it out to her as she rose up.

Acknowledgments

Thank you to the generous and encouraging Diane Goettel, and everyone at Black Lawrence Press, for giving my first book such a good home.

Thank you to Hamline University's MFA program, with special gratitude to Patricia Weaver Francisco and Deborah Keenan for seeing that I was on to something.

Thank you to the Loft Literary Center. From my first fiction class to my place in the Mentor Series, the Loft has been there—steadfast—making a way for writers just like me. And to the editors who have selected and helped shape my stories through the years.

Solidarity and thanks to my writing comrades, past and present, especially Alison Morse, Cullen Bailey Burns, Amy Fladeboe, and Kasey Payette. And to Samantha Bohrman and Cristina Pippa, new friends and indispensable writing allies.

Thank you with abundant love to my family. My mother, Julie Richardson—for so many things—including the gift of time to write when my children were very young. My son and daughter, Joey and Grace, for inspiring me to honor my creative work and to become a better human. And most of all, to my husband, Paul, for helping me get started, for seeing me through, and for having faith in me all along.

"Some Good News to Tell" appeared in a slightly different form as "Birdie, Birdie" in *The Threepenny Review*. "Don't Tell Your

Mother" appeared as "The Way to Mercy" in *The Sun Magazine* and was anthologized in *New Writing from the Midwest* with Swallow/Ohio University Press. "But I Will Tell You Otherwise" appeared as "The Story of Cha Cha McGee" in *American Fiction Volume 13* with New Rivers Press. "The Ghost of L.T. Bowser Tells What Really Went Down" appeared in a slightly different form as "A Postmortem Addendum from Mr. L.T. Bowser (1887-1969)" in *Walls You Can Read*, a commemorative anthology by The Soap Factory Gallery. "Let Her Tell the Way" appeared in a slightly different form as *Niagara Falls* with Red Bird Chapbooks. "When the Saints Tell Their Own" appeared as "Blue" in *Midway Journal*. "What the Universe Tells Marta" appeared in *Jet Fuel Review*. "Please Tell Us Your Beautiful Secret" appeared in *Emerging Writers Network*.

Photo: Mark Riddle

Beth Mayer's fiction has appeared in *The Threepenny Review*, *The Sun Magazine*, and *The Midway Review*. Her stories have been anthologized in *New Stories from the Midwest* (Ohio University/Swallow Press) and *American Fiction* (New Rivers Press), and have been recognized by *Best American Mystery Stories* among "Other Distinguished Stories." *The Missouri Review*'s 2016 Jeffrey E. Smith Editors' Prize in fiction named her a finalist and her work in *Jet Fuel Review* has been nominated for the 2017 Best of the Net. Beth holds an MFA from Hamline University, was a Loft Mentor Series Winner in Fiction for 2015–16, and teaches in the Minnesota State Colleges and Universities system. She lives in Minneapolis/St. Paul with her family and impossibly loyal dog.